MW01688663

Four on the Floor

And Other Quirky Stories for Our Time

Ross & Verna
This is for your grandchildren
1/18/01

Four on the Floor

And Other Quirky Stories for Our Time

Thomas Sebastian Fiske
With illustrations by
Caleb Fiske

FirstPublish, Inc.
Orlando, Florida

Copyright © 2000 by Thomas Sebastian Fiske.
Illustrations by Caleb Fiske
All rights reserved. Printed in the United States of America.
No part of this publication may be reproduced, stored in
a retrieval system, or transmitted, in any form or by any
means, electronic, mechanical, photocopying, recording,
or otherwise, without the prior written permission of the author.

ISBN
1-922925-30-1

Library of Congress Cataloging in Publication Data
00-110089

Thomas Sebastian Fiske
Four On the Floor
And Other Quirky Stories for Our Time

FIRSTPUBLISH, INC.
170 Sunport Ln. Suite 900
Orlando, FL 32809
407-240-1414
www.firstpublish.com

Dedication

To my long-suffering parents, Walter and Alice Fiske,

who sat through many all-night vigils

hoping and praying the boys would live another day.

They made my travails as a parent seem easy.

Contents

Acknowlegement

Some of these stories have never been published, but parts of others have appeared in magazines such as *Heritage Quest* and *Northern Kentucky Heritage*. Those stories are used with the generous consent of the publishers.

Most of the ideas in these stories are original with the author. Some of the History and Science stories came through constant reading over many years and searching through the Internet. Other stories are the result of listening to the usual tales that are told in families about their ancestors.

All the stories are as true as I can make them, based on research that was current when the stories were first created. If science and history have changed since the stories were researched, then the reader must make allowances.

But Holly, Jeff, Bob and Jim did have all the difficulties I have told about. Julie was killed ten years ago as this is being written. Those facts will never change.

Introduction

Scheherezade had it right. There is nothing like telling a story to get a person through a tough time. She had to tell a thousand and one tales but her skills kept her head on her shoulders for quite a while.

Just like Scheherezade, I found myself in front of tough audiences many times and used stories to distract people from their thoughts of violence against my person. In classrooms of students from graduate school to middle school, I managed to survive, to get a lesson across, and to return the next time without losing too much scalp. Unlike Scheherezade's tales though, all my stories are true.

Students, after hearing several stories in a semester, often came to the conclusion that I was cursed, or at least had a hard life. I never thought so. I felt blessed in my lifetime. It just seemed to me that sometimes bad things happen to all people, and no exception was made for me and my family. Some of those things were actually funny.

I did not live in an exotic spot like Brooklyn, New York, that so charmed the great story-teller, Sam Levenson. I had less to work with, having been brought up with two mean brothers in the South. We probably were not as poor as Sam was, but we were certainly not rich, by any means, except that we had thousands of acres of heavily wooded public parks to roam in. There we dreamed we were Daniel Boone-type pioneers. Not a whole lot of people have such an advantage.

There weren't many career openings for Daniel Boone-type pioneers, so I settled for positions in manufacturing, giving up my beloved forests for the insides of factories. There was a positive side even to this sacrifice: one cannot get poison ivy in a factory. It was only after I retired from the rigors of "factory arts" that I decided to fill some empty hours with teaching.

Not being an expert on every subject, I found it difficult to load all educational hours with a full schedule of activity. So I began to fill in blank spaces with stories about my children or my brothers. Eventually, I began to include odd-ball science and math stories, too.

Students wanted more (anything is better than studying). When they saw that I was substituting in their classrooms, they would demand a story before lessons began. Occasionally I would meet their parents, who seemed to know every detail of each story. They wanted to know more, and that is the reason for this book.

My collection of stories is both for adults and kids. There is often a moral for each one. I mean for each story to be edifying or educational (there is a difference).

Caleb, an artist of some fame in St Petersburg, Florida, took each story, and without any direction from me, made an illustration that appealed to him. Thus, the illustrations reflect his own views and creativeness. They are not necessarily what I would have produced if I were the artist; they are far better and more imaginative.

So, have at it. If you don't know the importance of fingertips, you have a lot of reading to do.

PART ONE

Kids and Other Disasters

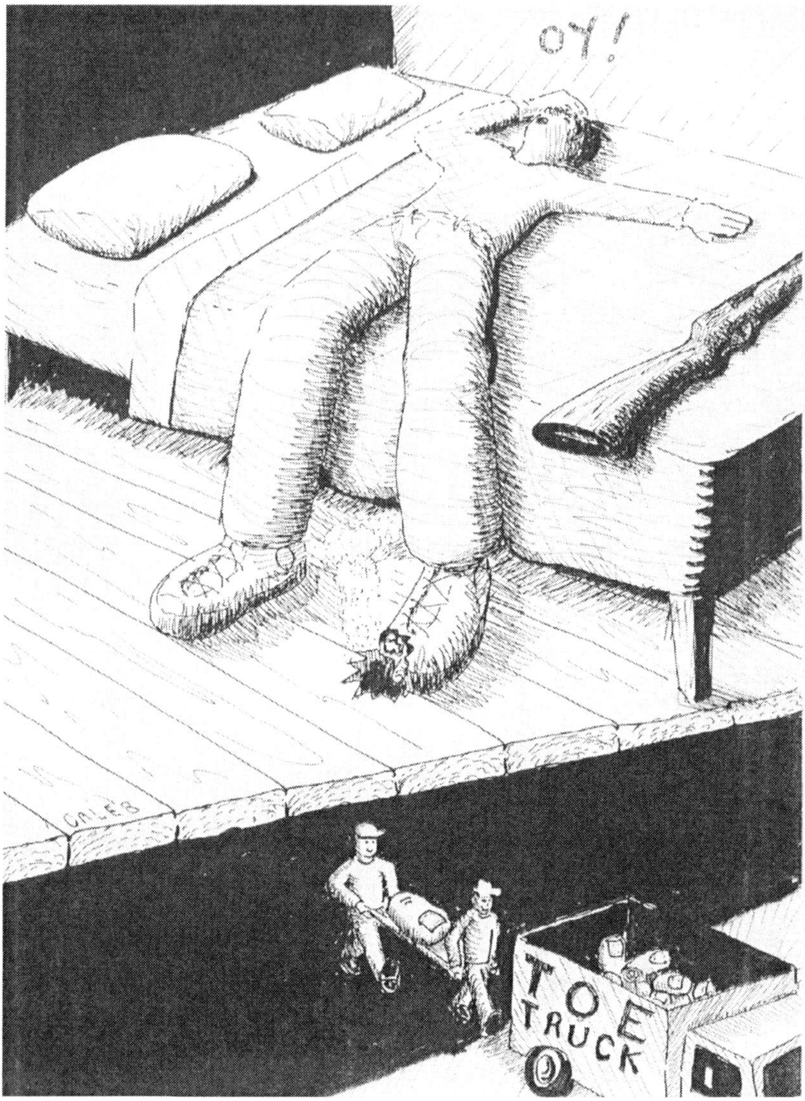

One way to get "Four on the Floor."

Four on the Floor

(Or, How My Wonderful Brother Blew His Toe Off)

How many stories begin with, "Now, when I was your age"? Well, I am not going to do that. I am just going to mention that I was one of the younger Radio Ham Operators in the Country. Not the youngest, but one of them. I was, maybe, in eighth grade.

One evening I was building a radio transmitter in my room. I loved to do that. Of course, I was ignoring my math homework, but the transmitter was needed that night, while the homework was only due the next day.

While I was puzzling over a wiring diagram and wishing to be completely alone, in came my wonderful big brother, Jim.

Now, you may have a wonderful big brother or sister like I had. He was

Bigger
Smarter
Wiser
Funnier
Better Looking
More Artistic
And

he made better grades in school than I did. It was tough living up to the standard of my big brother. I knew I would never make it if I kept on building radios, but somehow I couldn't stop.

Anyway, Jim was holding something as he came into my room. In his right hand he had a shotgun. In his left hand he had a shotgun shell. There were three of us boys and we all had guns, so what Jim had was not exceptional.

The shotgun shell *was* a bit exceptional, though. It was old. Our father purchased it at least twenty-five years previously. It had been stored in the attic, and at one time the roof leaked on it. In short, the shell was lumpy. It looked like a lipstick tube with mumps.

"I wonder if this thing will fit?" my wonderful brother said, trying to engage me in conversation. I said nothing.

While I sat with a soldering iron in my hand, trying to figure out where the next wire went, I heard the click-click of the pump action of the gun, and I knew the shell had indeed fit. This is a satisfying sound to a man as the well oiled and precision parts of a fine gun slide against each other and fall into place.

After several other attempts to get my attention failed, my wonderful brother walked out of the room with his gun still in hand.

It must have been only two minutes later that I heard the gun go off.

You have to realize that when a sixteen gauge shotgun goes off in a wood frame house, you immediately are aware of it. The walls shake, your eardrums hurt, the people next door know about it and dogs down the street start howling. It is simply something you can't ignore.

So, I put down my soldering iron and dashed back to his room. The room smelled like burned gun powder. Wisps of blue smoke curled through the air. Peering through the smoke I saw him. He was lying on his back and one arm was thrown outward. His eyes were shut tight. The other hand was on his forehead.

I knew something terrible had happened. In fact, I was sure that if I pried his cold hand from his forehead, I would see a half inch hole there where the full charge of a sixteen gauge blast had torn through his skull. So sure was I of what happened, that I looked at the wall behind him to see the blood, brains and bits of bone that should be there as the blast dug itself in the plaster.

But they weren't there!

Suddenly Jim spoke. He said "Oy, It shuddent heppen to ha dawg!" He had a funny accent he used when telling jokes. I said he was funnier than I was.

"What shouldn't happen to a dog?" I asked in my horrified voice.

"I shot myself in the foot," he exclaimed.

Now when a public speaker shoots himself in the foot, he has said something that was self-defeating that may cause an audience to lose confidence in him. But this is not what my wonderful brother meant. He really shot himself in the foot!

I looked down at his shoe. There on the top of his leather shoe was the half inch hole I expected to find in his forehead.

You need to know that when a shotgun fires, its shot begins to expand. Therefore, the first hole it makes close to the barrel is small, about the size of the bore. Then, when the shot hits something farther out it makes a larger hole, and so on.

The bottom of my brother's shoe was almost blown off. It was hanging by a thread, and every time his pulse beat, the dangling sole would swing in the smoke-filled air.

There was a hole in the wood floor, under his shoe, about two inches in diameter. And my wonderful brother's big toe was in the hole. That toe is still there for all I know. It has been about forty years since it all happened and I didn't remove it.

Well, think about it: If you are groping around under the floor boards of an old house, there are several things you don't want to find. One is a dead rat. They are squishy and they smell bad and carry diseases. Another is a live snake. They bite when frightened. And the last thing you want to find is your brother's big toe.

I just pushed a rug over the hole.

And you know how fathers are. Mine was downstairs wondering what was going on. So he did the usual—he yelled upstairs, "WHAT THE HECK IS GOING ON UP THERE? He didn't really say, "Heck," either. Freely translated he was saying, "I'm busy, I don't want to come up there and discipline anybody, so stop it."

Dad yelled this message up the steps many times, but only once did I ever have an appropriate answer. This time I said loudly, "Jim shot himself in the foot."

With that, my father calmed down and quickly called our family doctor. This medicine man said not to worry, that gunshot wounds didn't bleed much. We were to wrap his foot and bring Jim to the hospital. I got under one arm and our father got under the other arm, and we helped my wonderful brother to the car and to the the emergency room.

In the hospital that day my wonderful brother began paying three penalties for his mistake. First, it hurt when the doctor pulled a flap of skin up over the stump and sewed it all back together, with a tube stuck inside so it could drain.

Second, Jim was moved to a room for a week with a Southern Baptist preacher. Now, I'm not saying anything bad about these ministers. I am just saying that Jim was an Episcopalian who particularly disliked Baptist preachers. That week he learned a lot more about Jesus and the Bible than he ever wanted to know.

The third penalty was more obvious. Every time you take a step, you end the step by pushing off with a big toe. That is the way you learned and you never think about it. What do you do when you lose a big toe? You walk on the side of your foot for the rest of your life. You have a strange kind of limp. And that was what Jim was forced to do for the rest of his years.

Every day in each large city, several people are hurt when *unloaded* guns go off. My wonderful brother confided in me that he had simply forgotten the shotgun was loaded. When you handle guns you have to check yourself and everybody else constantly so you know whether a gun is loaded or not. Many people are killed or maimed by "unloaded" guns. My wonderful brother was lucky. His forgetfulness could have killed him or put him in a wheelchair.

Actually, my wonderful brother suffered one more penalty. We kidded him a lot. In those days we boys loved our hot rod automobiles. We could put any kind of transmission and any kind of engine into a car that would fit. Then we would race our creations down the back roads of our cities to see how fast we could go.

Our favorite gear shift arrangement was called "four on the floor." This meant a manual gear shift lever that came out of the floor boards. It worked a gear box that had three gears forward and one in reverse: four on the floor.

Of course, whenever anyone said "four on the floor," we pointed to my wonderful brother's right foot and snickered. He had, on that foot, four on the floor. He had blown the fifth toe off for good.

My wonderful brother was wonderful in every way except that he couldn't remember that he had loaded a gun. He may have been

Bigger
Smarter
Wiser
Funnier
Better Looking
More Artistic
And
he made better grades in school than I did.

But forty years later, I have all my toes.

As Holly drifts around in a small swimming pool, she lines up in a north-south direction because of the needle in her foot.

Dad, I have a Needle in my Foot!

You know how sometimes science lectures go in one ear and out the other? Well, one day I was a student in a seventh grade science class and it was a warm day. The windows were open, flies were buzzing around, and somewhere a baseball team was playing hard. I could tell every time someone hit the ball because I heard the hit and then the echo as its sound reverberated off the brick wall of our school building. Of course, people cheered, and the chatterbox who goes to all games, was telling everybody his job: "Attaboy, Charlie, you can do it boy," and so on. All in all, it was a difficult day to be in school.

But somehow, the teacher's remarks went in one ear and stopped somewhere about my left eye. They stayed with me. I don't know why, because my mind was really on the long-ball hitter.

The teacher was talking about magnetism, and you need to know what she was saying if you are going to understand my story.

First, she said the Earth had a core of iron. Some was molten and some was not. Anyway, she said the iron was magnetic and gave out huge lines of force that came out of the North Pole and went in the South Pole. The Chinese, about four hundred years ago, discovered that if they floated a thin sliver of iron in a bowl of water, the sliver would line itself up in a north-south direction. This was handy on cloudy days and nights, because one could navigate without stars or the Sun.

The western world found out about this discovery and used it later, but it was the Chinese who invented the device which we now call a compass.

The teacher demonstrated the "sliver" compass by sticking an ordinary needle through a piece of cork and floating it in a beaker of water. It worked every time.

Then the teacher took a real compass from her desk. It had a needle on a pivot in a brass case complete with letters all over its face, showing in great detail where everything was. She also took out a permanent magnet. When she held the magnet close to the compass, its needle spun around to the magnet and tried to jump out of the case.

The teacher said the Earth was just a big magnet and compass needles all over the world are attracted to it. It was amazing how the needle tried to jump out of the case, though.

Now, on to my story. It was about ten in the evening, bedtime for my daughter, Holly. She was in the eighth grade, as I recall. She came to me in her bare feet and said, "Dad, I think I have a needle in my foot."

It was a matter of fact statement, so I answered the same way: "What makes you think you have a needle in your foot?"

"Well," she said in her best scientific manner, "I lost the needle I was working with. Then, when I was walking across the carpet, I felt a stabbing pain in my foot. Finally, I have a small hole in the bottom of my foot."

That was pretty good evidence, but it was only circumstantial. Taking Holly's small foot in my hand, I looked at the bottom of it. Sure enough, there was a small hole in the area just below her toes. I did what any loving dad would do: I twisted her foot in a mean spiral. "Does that hurt?" I asked her.

"Well, a little," she responded.

I bent her foot forward, sharply. "How about this?"

"Yes. Some," Holly said with tears in her eyes.

I bent her foot backwards. "How about now?"

"Not real bad," she said bravely, as she wiped the tears from her face.

Suddenly remembering my seventh grade science, I said, "Holly would you get me a large permanent magnet?" She limped off to locate a large magnet I had taken from a loudspeaker and stored in the basement.

When Holly returned with the magnet, I put her foot in my lap and held it with my left hand. Then with my right hand holding the magnet, I ran it across the bottom of her foot. She screamed. Maybe she had a needle in there but I wasn't sure, so I ran it across the opposite direction. She screamed in pain once again.

Two out of two wasn't bad. According to my science teacher the needle was trying to jump out of Holly's skin and attach itself to the magnet. As it jumped in her foot, it must have nudged a nerve and upset her somewhat.

At this point, I said, "O.K., Holly, I think it is time to visit the emergency room at the hospital." She got dressed in her "going to the emergency room clothes." She had been there many times, and this was no big deal to either one of us.

When we arrived and signed in, a doctor looked at the forms we filled out and said, "O.K., Holly, what is it this time?' I don't know why doctors go to the trouble of reading the forms and then ask the same questions the forms ask, but they do.

"I have a needle in my foot," was the reply.

"Then maybe you should go to the x-ray department so we can have a look." With that, the doc asked an orderly to put Holly in a wheel chair and push her to the x-ray room, which he did. We waited for about fifteen minutes.

Here came Holly, being wheeled back, and she had a lap full of x-rays. The doc picked up the first one and said, "Uh huh, here it is!" He held it up so I could see, and sure enough, a needle about two inches in length was buried deep in Holly's foot. It ran from north to south, that is, toes to heel, and it was buried deeply.

Holly had a look at the x-ray, and the orderly had a turn at scanning them also. He nodded wisely as he spotted the metal. Looking at me for approval, the doctor said perhaps he should operate. I nodded and wondered if she would have to be admitted to the hospital. The doc said that he could operate in the emergency room and that Holly could go home afterwards.

That was the good news. Then the doc said those words that you don't want to hear. You really want to know you are O.K. and can go home, but the doc says, "Get up on the table." These are five bad words.

Holly climbed up on a table that was equipped with wheels. She lay on her stomach while the doc got out two hypodermic syringes, a scalpel, and several other devices.

The doc gave her two shots. One was for tetanus. The needle in her foot might have germs. Tetanus germs could lead to a serious infection that could cause her to lose a leg or might even kill her. Those shots hurt some.

Then Holly got a shot for pain. Not for the pain she had, but for the pain she was going to have. With the skill of an artist, the doctor painted the bottom of Holly's foot with a red antiseptic solution. Then he picked up the scalpel.

With great precision (I watched every move) the doctor placed the point of his scalpel above the spot on her foot where the needle had gone in. Then he plunged the blade into her foot and pulled down a distance of two inches. She did not bleed much.

The inside of Holly's foot looked like Lobster Tail. That's right—it was white stuff that wiggled in places as she moved her toes. Of course, Holly couldn't see what was happening and she could not feel anything, so she didn't care what the doctor did.

But I cared. I was getting nervous. No right-thinking father wants to see his little daughter get cut up. It made me very nervous. Sometimes when I am under a lot of pressure, I say funny things to help relieve it.

The doc reached into the wound with a great deal of sureness and a pair of some kind of pliers. He rummaged around for a bit and the smiled as he pulled out a huge needle.

"Well, there it is," he said proudly as if he had just landed an eight pound bass from a lake in Kentucky. He showed it to me and then put it and the pliers down. "Holly," he continued, "you will have to go back to x-ray so we can be sure there is no more metal in your foot. I don't want to sew you up and have to go back inside later."

"O.K.," Holly said, not aware of the mess I saw at the other end of her portable table. She didn't care if school let out at recess. Nothing was bothering her.

There was no more metal, so the doctor began to sew her up. As you might imagine, it was just a matter of jabbing a curved needle through the edges of the would and pulling a thread tight to close it up.

After a couple of stitches, the doc decided to involve me in some conversation. I wasn't saying much at this point, wishing that he was operating on me and not Holly. "Dad (he referred to me as Dad because he wasn't interested in names, just wounds), how did you know that the needle was actually in her foot?"

I was really nervous at this point. I said, "Well, Doc, I filled the bath tub with water. Then I put Holly's leg in it ten times. Nine times out of ten her foot swung North."

This really broke him up. He laughed and laughed. The he said, "You're lying, aren't you?"

I said I was and told him about the trick with the magnet. The doc said that was the first time he ever heard of that technique. He thought he might be able to do something like that in the emergency room.

And then I realized that the long arm of my science teacher, many years ago, had just reached into the emergency room of that hospital, two thousand miles away. A little science goes a long way, doesn't it?

Having stitched up his little patient, the doc had me fill out some forms. He got a crutch for Holly with some pain pills and sent us on our way home.

That should be the end of the story, but this is Holly we are talking about so there is more.

About one month after the operation, Holly went to her own doctor to get her stitches removed. It was a bit early, but she wanted to go to the eighth grade dance, she explained, and the stitches bothered her.

The kindly doctor removed Holly's stitches, which was a great relief for her. It hurt some to get them out but Holly thought it was worth the pain. After all, they had to come out some time, she reasoned, and it might as well be now.

As soon as the stitches were out, Holly stood up to see how it would feel. It was then, when all her weight was on the injured foot, that the entire wound opened up! It had never healed.

The doctor told Holly that he could not stitch her up again. The sides of the wound were too weak to hold the sutures. She would have to be on crutches for six months more, and would have to let the wound heal from the inside out.

So Holly did not get to go to the dance.

And that should be the end of the story, but this is Holly we are talking about, so there is more.

Recently I was talking with Holly and I discussed the story with her to see if the facts were essentially correct. She said they were, but that I had left out the best part of the story. I didn't know there was a "best" part!

But there definitely was. During the next six months in junior high school, Holly said she never had to carry a book. The eighth and ninth grade boys felt sorry for the small blond girl, and *they* carried her books. The school was on two floors and they even carried her up and down the stairs. Holly said she never had so much attention in her life as when she was on crutches for those last six months.

It seems that when things look bad there is sometimes some good coming out of the bad. Whatever the outcome, you have to listen HARD in science class because you never know when you hear something that will help you raise your children.

Jeff takes his first flight

Tough Breaks

One fine day my son, Jeff, was out riding around on his bicycle, having a great time showing himself and the world how he could perform minor miracles on two wheels. He was in the fourth or fifth grade, as I recall. His demonstration wasn't completed, however, until gravity showed its ugly force and managed to upset Jeff in an untimely way.

No, it wasn't untimely because he fell. It was untimely because he was not supposed to fall when he was wearing his good pants. Actually, he was supposed to have changed his clothes before he went riding, but he was in a big hurry, and such action completely slipped his mind. You know how that can happen.

During the collapse, Jeff limited damage to two areas: his right arm, and his new pants. By protecting himself with the arm he managed to avoid severe damage to his head. And by deftly allowing his new pants to take the brunt of the fall, he had to sacrifice only one knee in them. The rest of the new pants were hardly touched by the accident. Of course, he managed to avoid a terrible scrape in the same area of his leg.

Well, Jeff managed to drag himself home and take the terrible tongue lashing from his mother about the new pants. We parents were young, with two children, and we were well aware that money was hard to come by. Of course, Jeff complained about his arm and how sore it was. But the noise of the complaint was lost to the terrible silence that followed. A boy should follow his parents' instructions about changing his clothes before going out to play.

Jeff said the arm did not feel right. But his mother was working in a hospital and saw people every day who came in with the silliest of complaints. She wasn't going to take her son there unless there was something really wrong. The arm looked OK to her. She knew that broken arms swell around the break and this one didn't swell, so it was only sprained or something.

It was a couple weeks later when the episode about the torn pants was beginning to be forgotten, that Jeff came down with a cold. It soon turned into bronchitis. Jeff had a history of this kind of problem.

And by the way, parents (oh, I know you don't have children. But you will have children and I need to alert you to something now, before it is too late) you need to know that when children are small, they sometimes have breathing difficulties. There is nothing like sitting up all night in a shower stall with a sleepy, crying baby who has a hard time breathing unless the hot water is on and steam is infiltrating his air passages. You think each breath is going to be his last. It gives one time to think whether adding another child to the world's population is really worth all the bother.

We had a small family.

Well, eventually, we had to take Jeff to his pediatrician about the congestion in his lungs. While he and his mother were describing the symptoms to the doctor, Jeff insisted that the doctor look at his arm, which was still hurting from the time he fell off his bike.

After taking care of the congestion and prescribing various nostrums that were popular in those days, including antibiotics, the doctor took Jeff's arm in his capable hands. He asked where it hurt. It took only one test and the doctor said, "Um, better have this arm x-rayed." He kind of looked at us with a "How could you ignore this?" glare that only parents can understand.

Guiltily, we looked at our son. Jeff had the same look on *his* face.

So we went to the emergency room of our local hospital and had the arm x-rayed. Sure enough, one of the bones was fractured. Jeff was elated. Finally he was going to get some relief for his sore arm! He got a cast that went to, but not over, his elbow. That meant he had some flexibility. And he had a kind of "Badge of Courage" to show the other kids at school.

The good news was that the arm was partially healed, so the cast could come off in about four weeks. The bad news was that we had waited too long after the accident; our insurance would not cover the cost of the treatment. So we had to pay that, too.

And then there was a new problem. Jeff had wanted to take a special art class at his school. It cost twenty dollars and it was non-refundable. What to do? This was a class that involved much water, and Jeff's new cast wasn't like the nice light casts we have today: water would ruin it. We figured that he could use his arm a bit, so he might learn something from the class.

At the hospital Jeff's mother found a very good solution. She knew a sympathetic intern who had children and who understood the problem.

He donated some of those latex gloves that doctors use to investigate the various openings of the human body. They were plenty large enough for Jeff to get his hand in, and they also were long enough to cover the first few inches of his cast, so it would not get wet.

And the solution worked! Every day Jeff went off to his art class with the "special" glove over his hand and cast. The class must have been beneficial because today he is quite good as an artist and is illustrating these stories. His arm still hurts, but he does not wear those gloves. And, he manages to keep both knees in his pants, so I hear.

If you have really good eyes you can see that the road leads to Sacramentoe

Weird Connections

One of the reasons we grow frustrated with school is that sometimes the materials we study seem unrelated to anything we do or will be doing in the real world. And this may be true.

However, we have to consider the unreal world before we give up entirely on our lessons.

By unreal world, I mean what goes on in our heads as our minds develop and grow and we become adults. Our brains are always working, whether we are asleep or awake, and they are constantly trying to make sense of the world we see everyday. One way our brains do this is to make connections between what we know and what we know only in part. When our brains do this, they sometimes make new constructions, which we call creative thinking.

Here are two examples:

The Toe Truck

Every family can point to examples like the ones I am about to use. The first one has to do with making connections through the use of word sounds. My kids, Holly and Jeff, were three years apart. Obviously, they were not twins but they had a special way of understanding each other that was foreign to their parents.

One day when Jeff was, maybe seven, and Holly was four, they were laughing over some remark I made about our car, which had suddenly become sick. Its troubles became so bad that I had to have it taken to the repair shop. A tow truck, I explained, had to come and take it away.

I didn't see anything funny about our situation, but Jeff and Holly continued to giggle. Somewhat irritated, I asked what was so funny. Jeff said that he and Holly thought I was talking about a TOE truck, and they were imagining a large dump truck full of human toes. The thought of such a vehicle going down the street made them laugh out loud.

They were right. It was a funny idea, on the ridiculous side, and for a moment, I was able to laugh with them.

The kids made a connection between the two kinds of trucks because of the way the words sounded. But there are other connections, too.

Madder than a Wet Beezoe

This other type of connection, and I suspect there are many types, will make my point even stronger.

Our small family usually had a good time at dinner. The four of us would sit around the table and would talk about fun things that happened during the day. Jeff was maybe nine or ten years old and Holly was six or seven when Holly said about someone, "He was madder than a wet beezoe."

The expression I had always heard and her mother had always heard was "Madder than a wet hen." It is a farming expression, meaning that chickens don't like to get wet, and sometimes they fuss a great deal when they are sprinkled with rain or a hose. People are like that. They fuss a lot when something goes wrong. So it is natural for a farmer to say about someone, "Madder than a wet hen."

But we couldn't figure out what Holly was saying. For a minute. Then her brother burst out laughing. He figured it out. I was mystified, but I knew there was some logic to the statement. Holly explained. It was perfectly simple to her and she didn't see why the rest of us didn't get it.

The week before, at the dinner table, Jeff had been talking about his friend Del, a boy who lived down the street. Del had gone to summer camp for years. At summer camp in the evening after dinner, the boys and girls would sit around a campfire and sing songs. One of their favorites had an ending that Del never understood. But he sang it anyway. The last words of the song, as Del heard them, were, "And never wash your beezoe."

Well, Del learned the real words eventually, and he told Jeff what they were: "And ever more shall be so." But that line, when sung, sounded like, "And never wash your beezoe." He was just a kid and didn't question the words that sounded so strange.

So, what is a Beezoe? This drawing may be the only depiction in existence

Jeff took that story to the dinner table and we laughed about it. Then a week later Holly said, someone was "madder than a wet beezoe." We didn't understand that she made a connection between the expression "madder than a wet hen," and an unwashed beezoe that never got wet, but surely would be angry if it ever did get wet. When we heard part of the explanation, the entire idea snapped into place for all of us. We all had a great laugh. The connection had been made.

There was a connection because of the way the words sounded. Also there was a more complex connection between an old farm expression, a song whose words were not understood, and a method of making a family laugh. It was the family sense of humor. When a six year-old girl put all these things together, she got a reward. It was her family's approval and acceptance. She was the youngest child and the one who wanted to show she could be a full-fledged contributing member of the family.

All that information we learn in school! It seems useless sometimes. But during our lives it helps our minds make connections. The connections help us solve problems and create new things. The connections are being made while we are awake or even, I am told, while we are asleep. And the only limits are that we do not have enough information on which to build new bridges between new thoughts.

The playful creativeness of the human mind does all sorts of things when we let it do its magic. Unfortunately as we get older, we let that part of our personality grow small until it finally withers away. That's too bad, really. We need it as adults when we have the power and resources to bring creative ideas into being. Perhaps it is the artists, inventors, and musicians among us who manage to cling to their playful creativeness.

Some of the most boring people in the world have stopped learning. The work of their brains in making connections slows down. Their brains are starved for information, and they just repeat what they have said in the past until no one wants to hear it anymore. Not only do they bore people but also they don't make as much money as they might, if they were more creative.

After all, people pay us to solve problems and create new things. If we want to be successful all our lives, our education will never cease. We will be students until the day we die. And we will be interesting people until that day, too.

Snake watches TV while Jeff's mother boils

The Great Snake Hunter

Everybody knows I love science. But I do not carry my love too far. I am not an Indiana Jones type. But my son is. Well, he used to be.

There was a man who wrote highly interesting books about snakes, back in the good old days. His name was Raymond Ditmars. His books are still available today. I read those books and, as a Boy Scout, I had a finely developed interest in snakes.

There were lots of snakes to look at in Kentucky. It is a green, heavily wooded state. Copperheads, rattlesnakes, cottonmouths, milk snakes, and garter snakes were only a few of the many we had in our woods and sometimes around our homes. We ordinary people needed to know which were the helpful snakes and which were the dangerous snakes. The helpful ones killed rodents and unwanted insects. The dangerous ones were poisonous. The shape of the animal's head often told whether he was poisonous. So we tried to learn about snakes to encourage the one kind and discourage the other.

And when I had a son, what did I tell him about? My most satisfying interests. Jeff quickly learned about snakes and became a font of much more knowledge than I ever had. He consulted Ditmar's books plus many others. Then he decided to go looking for samples. Live ones.

Jeff tried many mechanical methods of capturing snakes with long sticks that have loops of wire on the ends. But somehow they were too much trouble. I didn't know it at the time, but he managed to find a better way to capture them: he would go crashing into the brush and grab them behind the head with his bare hand. He would drop them into a pillow case and worry about poisons later.

We lived in Cleveland, Ohio, at the time. I can just see the Cleveland snakes looking over their shoulders and moaning, "Lookout! Here comes Jeff again!"

One day Jeff was looking all over the house for a goldfish bowl. You know, it is one of those round glass things that you put goldfish in until you forget to change the water and they die. We had an old one around the house, and that was what he wanted. He found it and put some brush inside. Then he put a light metal top over it, to contain the garden snake he had recently caught. He kept the snake in his room, but he didn't tell anyone else.

One day we saw Jeff rooting around the house, obviously looking for something.

"What are you looking for?" his mother asked.

"Oh, I had a snake in my room and it got out," he said rather matter-of-factly."

His mother was not a bit happy about the fact that a snake was roaming around the second floor of her home, and she told Jeff so. I joined in the lecture and helped him look for the reptile.

We didn't find the snake. I estimated that an enterprising young snake could find a crack in the floor boards in our old house and could sneak outside on his own. Eventually, everything settled down.

Two weeks later Jeff's mom was sewing a dress for our daughter. She had the TV on for company. Something moved and she saw it out of the corner of her eye. It was the snake, which appeared out of nowhere, and was watching a commercial on the TV set.

Jeff's mother wasn't silly about snakes, but she really didn't like them much. So she whistled a very strong whistle for Jeff to come in and take the snake out. He didn't hear her, so she tried yelling and then screaming. The snake was between her and the door.

Finally, she realized she was holding an important item: the material she was working on. So she tossed it over the snake and took off to look for Jeff. She found him and got him to go in and grab the snake. He took the snake to the back yard and let it go a lot sooner than his mother let go of the subject.

After the ensuing tongue-lashing, Jeff never again brought a snake into our house. I don't blame him one bit.

Then we moved. We went to New York. Now, when you think of New York, you think of tall buildings, lots of cars and no place to park. But that is a very small part of New York State. It is a large state full of trees and bushes, a great place for snakes. Jeff really liked it for that reason. He continued with his headlong pursuit of snakes and his secret method of shaking hands with them.

One Sunday afternoon Jeff and I were talking about something when I noticed some bite marks on his arm. They were a bunch of tiny teeth marks arranged in a semicircle.

"What's that?" I said as I pointed to the marks.

"Nothing. A snake bit me. I guess I grabbed him too far back from his head," Jeff explained with no emotion at all.

I was getting anxious. I could see from the teeth marks the snake wasn't supposed to be poisonous, but I wanted to be sure. Jeff noticed the concern in my eyes and he said, "Here, I'll show you the snake; it was in my snake book."

Sure enough, the snake in his book wasn't poisonous. But I said, "I need to see the snake to be sure."

Jeff had the snake in his pillow case and showed me. I was satisfied.

Then came the bad news: "Jeff, we'll have to go to the hospital and get you a tetanus shot."

Jeff hated shots and tetanus above all. He wanted to argue about it, kind of hoping we could wait until the arm began dropping off. Then he would get a shot.

But I wasn't having any of that. The snake might have bitten a rat with the plague just before he got Jeff. There is no reason to think that snakes brush their teeth after every meal. So, we took his snake book with us as we went to the local emergency room. Sure enough, as soon as the doctor hear the words, "Snake Bite," he wanted to keep Jeff in the hospital for observation. After all, the poor man probably was a city dweller and never had the pleasure of getting close to a snake.

We showed the doctor the book and the pictures and all, and eventually convinced him that Jeff was not poisoned by two fangs. Jeff got his shot and went home with a sore arm.

And that was the day his interest in snakes peaked out.

But you know, almost thirty years later, I still check pillowcases before I put them on the pillows.

Holly sees the value of a cast on one's arm

Two Arms and Three Elbows

(Or, Be Careful What You Pray For, You Might Get It)

This is another adventure with Holly. It began on a Sunday morning in church, when Holly, an eighth grader, was bored out of her skull with the sermon, and was concentrating on an injury her girlfriend at school had received. Of course, Holly told me all this much later. There was no way I could have known what was going through her mind.

The girlfriend had a slight fracture of her right arm, and with it she got a cast. The long white plaster surface was too much to resist, so immediately, it was filled up with names and signatures and slogans by the boys in her class. Holly saw all this and wished *she* might also get a cast so she could get some of that attention as well.

And that afternoon she got her wish.

After our Sunday dinner, Holly and a girl who lived across the street (I think her name was Laurie) toured the neighborhood. It was one of those warm days when there were no clouds in the very blue sky, and everybody felt a bit goofy with the beauty of it all. The girls went to a street where a contractor was building several new houses. Workers had graded the lots so they were flat and surfaced with soft brown earth. Between the lots there was a slight slope, because the lots were cut into a small downgrade.

Well, Laurie pushed Holly down one of the slopes. It was on soft ground and only a couple of feet down and it should not have hurt anyone. But this is Holly we are talking about, so something had to happen. Holly landed on a rock with her arm. Then her body landed on top of the arm, bending it sharply over the rock's curved surface. Everybody heard the sharp crack as the bones in Holly's arm broke.

Holly was hurting. She began to turn a bit gray, and Laurie saw that she wasn't able to walk on home. So she asked a young couple standing nearby if they would help her home. And they did.

The doorbell rang and there stood Holly with her mangled arm and a young couple behind her, explaining how it happened. It was very nice of them to take Holly home, but no one recalls what they said. All I could see was Holly's arm—it was horribly mangled with two elbows where there should have been only one. The broken bones gave her the appearance of a new elbow, as you must have figured out by now.

I brought her in and had her seated in a chair before she fell. Then I had a sling around her so she could not move the arm at all. I wanted to avoid any nerve damage that might occur (for many years I have been a Boy Scout and knew First Aid). Then I got her mother. The three of us drove to the Emergency Room of San Antonio Community Hospital in Upland, California, where Holly was a regular customer.

Business was slow that day, so a doctor saw Holly right away. He grimaced when he saw the arm. That should have been a warning to me, but it wasn't. After x-rays, we all went into the doctor's small office.

Now, in another story, I mentioned the words "get up on the table." I said these were the kinds of words you never want to hear from a doctor. Even your pet balks when the vet says them, such as "put the dog on the table." Those are bad words, all right. But there are worse words.

This time, the doctor looked at Holly's mother and said the worse words: "Would you please leave the room?" She caught on immediately and tears began to form in her eyes as she obediently walked away from us. Me, I'm fat dumb and happy. I didn't see the significance of his question until it was too late.

The doctor then said to me, "Will you please hold your daughter. I am going to finish breaking her arm."

Reluctantly, I put my arms around my small daughter and held her close to me while the doctor took her arm and pulled on it until there was another cracking sound and Holly almost keeled over.

Do you know who reminded me of this adventure? Yes, it was Holly, eighteen years later. She never forgot who held her while this was going on. She loves her mother, but she is still not too sure about me. Being a parent is not like being in a popularity contest. Often you have to do the very thing you do not want to do.

Well, Holly got her wish.

A fine, big cast was put on her arm. And we went home and that should be the end of the story. But this is Holly we are talking about, so there is more.

You know how it is when you break an arm or leg? You try out all kinds of moves so you can find your limitations. Holly was doing just that when she found a severe limitation. She came to me and said, "Dad, I can't close my fingers!"

Holly showed me that her thumb and forefinger would not touch. I was impressed but decided to try a real test on her. I put a dollar bill between her thumb and forefinger. I said she could have the money if she could hold on to it. Gently, the bill floated to the ground.

Then I gave Holly the supreme test, the kind only a loving father can administer. I put *ten* dollars between her thumb and forefinger. She perspired heavily and strained mightily, but the ten dollar bill gently floated to the ground. Twenty years ago, ten dollars was worth a lot to a fourteen year-old girl, more than it is worth today.

So Holly lost eleven dollars that day. We started back to her doctor to see what he could do about the damage to her arm. This time it was an orthopedic doctor, who specializes in broken bones and such stuff. He said that Holly had sustained nerve damage, and that happened frequently.

I am sure Holly realized that she got what she wanted, a broken arm and a cast, but it was much more complicated than she could have imagined.

The doctor said that sometimes it was helpful to operate on the nerves, and release pressure on them. I talked first with Holly and then said, "Go ahead." I didn't want Holly's arm to shrivel up through misuse. Yet the doctor said for us to wait for a while. Sometimes the nerves cured themselves and an operation wasn't necessary.

So we waited. Holly was very much involved with arts and crafts before her injury, but now it was all she could do to learn to write with her left arm. She wasn't able to sew or draw or paint anymore.

And we waited. Her right arm began to shrink as I feared. She used her left for just about everything. Still, the doctor recommended waiting.

After about a year, Holly came to me in the evening and showed me that she could hold a pencil. Some progress was being made, after all! Some weeks later she showed me she could hold a needle. I tested her again with money and she made eleven dollars. And finally the arm was back to normal. All she had to do was use it a lot and it would be the right size. Which she did.

I have not talked to Holly about that arm for twenty years. Recently, I called her and asked if it were all right. She said it was fine, but that she didn't have all the feeling back into her fingers, yet.

Well, I knew that was from the time a horse crushed the ends off her fingers. But that is a story for another day.

Some days you just wake up and your eyes don't want to work

The Day Holly's Eyes Went Bad

Today I am talking to you parents. Yes, you are parents even though you are still in school. You just don't have any children, yet.

The thought of living happily ever after never loses its appeal, does it? It doesn't matter how many troubles you see other people have. We were that way. To our family was born a happy, healthy little girl. We had a boy already, and we thought all we had to do was raise them, offering occasional guidance from time to time, until they took their turns at being president of the United States. But there is more to raising children than that.

Holly was three. That's a great age, for parents. Children are beginning to develop personalities, but they are still dependent on Mom and Dad. They sleep all night, have civilized bathroom habits, and are almost at the point of entertaining themselves. They aren't too heavy to pick up, and they will allow some hugs from time to time.

We had just put Holly to bed after a busy Sunday of working in a new church. Monday was on its way and all I had to do was go to work, which was a relief in a way.

The next morning promised to be the start of another week in which my wife and I fulfilled our duties to each other, the children, my employer, the famous General Electric Company, and to the Country. But it was to be no ordinary day.

The children got up as usual and made enough noise to wake us adults. We prepared a nice breakfast for our son who went to school, and for Holly, who was getting set for a big day with her toys and little friends next door.

But something was wrong. Holly's mother came in to the bedroom where I was putting on my tie. She had a strange, worried look on her face. "Something's wrong with Holly," she said, "You had better take a look."

At first Holly seemed just fine to me. She was playing with something at the breakfast table, but when she reached for her spoon, I noticed that she missed it. Her little hand closed on empty air. I said, "Holly, look at me."

Holly looked up and I immediately saw that one eye was looking left while the other one was looking right. It was a horrifying moment. When she went to bed she was fine, but when she woke, she was cross-eyed!

We poked and prodded her, looking for damage. We kept asking Holly if she were all right. She kept saying that she had no sore spots. It seemed that (a) she had poked herself in the eye, or (b) she had fallen and hit her head, causing brain damage.

I went on to work since she seemed to be in fine shape otherwise. Her mother called Holly's doctor as soon as she could, and took Holly to see him.

Holly's doctor was concerned, but could find nothing wrong with her. So he referred Holly to an ophthalmologist, a doctor who specializes in eye problems. He ran a bunch of tests and gave her some glasses designed to confuse her eyes so she would have to work hard with both of them in order to focus.

He also told us that there was nothing unusual going on, that children sometimes did this, and it was common. We had not heard of it, ever, and we called my mother in Louisville. She talked to my aunt who arranged for us to see a great neurologist who lived down there. We were in Cleveland, but he was in Louisville, and we made plane reservations.

This doctor was the one the Army flew to Germany after World War II to work on General Patton, when he was hurt in a vehicle accident. The fact that the General died did not deter us.

So we knew we had the best medical help we could get, anywhere. All we could do was wait. The specialists could find nothing wrong in Holly's small blond head. They noted that she seemed to be slow in developing, though. This was true, since she did not walk for several months after most children her age walked. And she was a small girl. The doctors seemed to think that Holly's developmental processes were not strong enough in the area of her eyes, and the control processes for the muscles that controlled her eyes were inadequate. They over-controlled, was the conclusion.

And so we tried glasses, which didn't help. We tried eye patches, where one eye was covered and the other one left open. Then we would reverse the process. During all this, Holly didn't complain. She was a good little patient.

After about a year our Cleveland doctor suggested surgery. He was getting very fond of Holly, and didn't want to do any damage, but it was the only procedure we hadn't tried. It didn't always work, he said. And even if it did, it might work for only a while.

We had faith in this kind, young doctor. And so we allowed him to operate. All he was going to do was cut a layer of optic muscle for both eyes so the muscles would not be as strong as they had been.

He operated. It was a one-day operation. You know what he did? He pulled Holly's right eye right out of her eye socket, reached in behind it with a scalpel, and then made a tiny cut in the muscle. Don't worry—the tissue has some stretch to it. Then he plucked the next eye out of its socket and repeated the same procedure. Holly was released from the hospital the same day she went in.

If you had seen this small blond girl you would have thought she was the worst looking fiend from the most awful horror movie ever made. The whites of her eyes were blood red. When she looked at something, her eyes seemed to be boring into it with a deadly ray. But her eyes were straight! That's what we saw. The operation was a success for that day and maybe for the rest of the year, and maybe until she got into junior high school!

By the way, we were informed that the bloody look was normal and that the red would disappear in a few days.

We would read to Holly at night while we watched her eyes. At the slightest hint of a wandering eye, we would put her to bed and turn the lights out. But each morning, her eyes were straight again.

And now, over twenty-five years later, we still ask Holly about her eyes. The answer is still the same: she is fine and so is her little daughter.

Holly's mother and I made the right decisions because we were educated parents. We went to good schools and learned something about biology. So you see, all this stuff you learn isn't just so you can pass tests. It is given to you to help you grow strong and healthy, and to help you help your children grow strong and healthy.

And when your children have children, you can yell at them for raising their kids incorrectly. That is great fun.

"Did the horse do that, too?" asked the judge, looking at Holly's crutch

Importance of Fingertips

If I asked any of you why fingertips were important, I bet you would not be able to tell me. After I tell you this story, you will know. It is another Holly story. I alluded to it when I told the Holly story about two arms and three elbows.

Holly and one of her girlfriends at school would ride horses at a stable near us in Upland, California. She was a seventh grader, I suppose. The other girl's parents and we would take turns dropping them off at the stable and picking them up later. They had the foothills of the San Gabriel Mountains to ride all over. There was a lot of open space and no cars to worry about.

One Saturday morning Holly said her friend could not go with her. We considered the facts and decided to take Holly up there anyway. She had been riding for a long time and should be able to handle herself.

I went on to work, leaving Holly's mother to handle the transportation problems. And when I got home there was a surprise waiting for me. Holly had a huge bandage on her hand.

"What happened to you?" I gasped.

"Got hurt by a horse today," Holly told me. She was afraid I would be angry with her.

It turned out that when Holly tried to rent her favorite horse, she was told by the stable owner that the horse was being ridden.

"Take number 5," he told her gruffly.

So Holly took number 5 and had a nice ride. When she came back and tried to tie up the horse, it reared. All thousand pounds of the horse pulled back. Unfortunately, Holly's small hand was in a steel ring, holding the reigns when it happened. Thus, her fingers were caught between the unyielding steel ring and the very heavy-duty reins. The result was that the ends of three of her fingers were crushed off.

Do you know what happens when you lose the ends of your fingers? The skin on your fingers falls back to your hand and what you see is muscle, tendons and bones. Holly lowered her hand and pulled the skin back over her fingers.

Then she went to the stable owner's shack to ask for help. He wouldn't give her any help, telling her to call her mother.

Well, it is difficult to dial a telephone when you have no fingertips. But Holly bravely managed somehow and her mother came to get her. They went directly to a hospital where plastic surgeons tried to fix as much of the damage as they could.

Holly's mother and I were furious at the stable owner for not helping. We wanted him to pay for Holly's medical bills. But he said, "No." Then Holly said something that really got my attention. She said, "As I was leaving the stable, a worker said, 'Number 5 always rears when you try to tie him up.'"

"Come on, Holly," I said, "we're going to see a lawyer." I was thinking that there was a point of law that might be in our favor. We explained our situation to the lawyer, and at the end I asked, "Do we have a case?"

The lawyer rubbed his hands together and smiled broadly. "Do we ever have a case!" he said.

I hate suing and courts, but this time I was really angry. So we filed lawsuit papers immediately. I found there is no advantage in threatening to sue; you just file the papers.

We waited for the case to come to court, and I am sure the other lawyer told his client to pay, that he was in deep trouble.

Well, the case finally came to court for a hearing. Holly walked into court with her mother and her lawyer. I was working again. Holly was on crutches. Her foot hadn't healed from the needle episode.

"Did the horse do that to her, too?" asked the judge, looking at her crutches.

Our attorney told the judge what had happened and the judge simply told the stable owner one word: "Pay."

Eventually a check came for Holly to be held in trust until she was eighteen.

What was the point of law? Well, if you put someone in danger, you have to tell him or her about it. If you had reason to believe a horse would unexpectedly rear, you have to tell the renter of the horse, or you are at fault. If you sell a car with bad brakes you have to tell the buyer the car has bad brakes or you, the seller, are responsible for what happens. It is the legal and ethical thing to do.

And what is the importance of fingertips? Fingertips keep the skin of your fingers from falling down.

Sudddenly the boys fell silent and gathered around my brother

One-Eyed Bob

For some reason toes are funny, but eyes are very serious. People laugh at the story (Four on the Floor) about my brother, Toeless Jim, but they get very quiet when I tell about my other brother, One-eyed Bob.

When was it? Oh, a long time ago when I was about seven, I guess. Mom and Dad shipped Jim and me off to our aunt's farm. I remember it was hot and we didn't miss any school. I guess it was summer. I also recall we city boys really enjoyed being farmers for a week or two. But there was an element of pain behind it all, of uncertainty. My Dad was deadly serious and was obviously hurting when he talked with us during that summer. And it wasn't until I had children myself that I could begin to understand what he was going through.

Jim was four years older and my idol. Bob was two years older and the bane of my existence. But when it came to neighborhood battles, we all joined together to defeat "the enemy." We had no *real* enemies, but there were some boys from down the street and a few blocks over with whom we had mock battles. We dressed alike and even looked alike and the only real differences between us may have been that they were Catholic and we were Protestant, or maybe it was Presbyterian and Episcopalian, but there were hardly any major differences.

Yet, we somehow found things to battle about. It was probably just "something to do" when everybody is bored in the mornings when it isn't too hot to venture out in the neighborhood.

Our grandmother offered to pay us a nickel or some small amount to go to Vacation Bible School. She could tell that our religious education was lacking, and beside, we were wasting valuable time. The conversion of time into Bible verses was not appealing, so we elected to hang around the neighborhood and see if we could find trouble. Eventually, in a dusty alley behind our house, we found it.

Why it was that we all had wooden swords I do not recall. Maybe some of us had sticks, but they were almost as good for swashbuckling as wooden swords. Anyway, the gang of Fiske boys and some others met with the gang of boys from down the street and the fight was on. We clashed swords and yelled and swore and chased and were chased for several minutes, when all of a sudden a hush fell over the crowd, and a circle of kids gathered around my brother, Bob. He was holding his face, his sword on the ground at his side.

The sudden silence told more than any words man has yet put together. Blood ran from between the fingers on my brother's face. Quickly the gang disappeared, and parents came out, and Bob was taken off somewhere. All we heard was whispering.

That night, Bob was still not home. At bedtime, Dad came to my bed and said that Bob had a splinter in his eye and was at a hospital. I knew it was serious when he said, "I wish it had happened to me rather than him." Then he asked for my help, and said he had arranged for Jim and me to go to stay "for a few days" at Aunt Queenie's farm.

We were afraid of Aunt Queenie but loved her farm, so this was good news. Uncle Bert was a well-to-do oral surgeon, and he was a gentleman farmer who lived just outside the city limits on a 64 acre dairy farm that was modern in every way. There were horses, mules, cattle (of course) fields of corn, and best of all, a pond to investigate. We loved that pond with all its frogs, snakes and dragonflies. Having to stay at the farm was one of the greatest gifts we could have been given.

We were there about two weeks. We learned to feed the livestock, to take out and ride the mules, to not step in the crusty cow pies (that was a difficult lesson), and generally to read conditions around us by watching birds and seeing how breezes moved tree limbs. The only hard thing we had to do was learn to drink milk fresh from cows, chilled a bit, but lumpy, and not at all like the smooth liquid we got from stores.

It would have been the high spot of our young lives if there were no problem at home. We weren't told about the fate of our brother. All we noticed were whispers and sad looks. Nobody was talking.

Finally our adventure was over and we came home to find our brother with a bandage over part of his face. Then we were told that the surgeon was able to save his eye but not the sight in it. Over time, Bob healed somewhat. After a while we all forgot the incident. Even he was used to seeing out of only one eye.

But we never knew what happened at home during those two weeks, never knew what Hell our parents went through, not only because a son lost the sight in an eye, but also because there were huge debts to be paid in a time when money was scarce.

Mostly what I, a seven year-old, could remember was the sudden silence, the circle of kids around my brother, and him holding his face while blood seeped from between his fingers. It all came back a quarter of a century later when my three year-old daughter suddenly required surgery on her eyes.

Yep, toes are definitely funnier than eyes.

PART TWO

Strange History

Even a dead Jesse James is popular

Digging Up Jesse James

For some years, now I have been digging into my family history. It is called a study of Genealogy. That's where some of my stories come from., you know.

Well, one day I came across an ancestor named Ann Marshall Samuell. She was the mother of the man who had to take the pledge never to try to divide the Country again, after the War Between the States, in 1866. Ann had an Uncle, Reuben Samuell, whose wife died. So, he married again. This second wife was a widow who had three children. Her name was Mrs. Zerelda James, whose children were Frank, Jesse, and Elizabeth. Reuben became the step-father of the children.

The two boys got involved in the War Between the States in 1861. They were on the losing side. After the war they decided to keep their guns and see what else they could do with them besides shoot Yankees. They had been battling in Missouri so they stayed and formed a gang with some of their fellow soldiers.

The James gang held up banks and trains in the Missouri area. They should have been easily caught, except for one thing. The people of Missouri, farmers and small townspeople, didn't care much for the owners of the banks and the railroads. Anyone who caused those people grief was fine in their books. So they helped the gang members hide from the police.

"Jesse who?" they would say, all the time hiding him in a back room, "Why, I don't think I have seen such a person."

The governor of Missouri finally offered a big reward for Jesse James—ten thousand dollars, dead or alive. By this time, Jesse had about dropped out of the robbery business. He was living at the home of a friend, Bob Ford, in a small town in Missouri. With him were his wife Zee and his two boys. One day, Jesse decided he couldn't stand to see a crooked picture on a wall. He got up to straighten it. While he had his back turned to his friend, Ford shot him in the head so he could collect the reward money. Some friend!

Well, people came from miles around to see the body of Jesse James. Others wrote songs and stories about him. About ten movies have been made, thirty books written and many songs composed about Jesse. You may have heard some of them. One is currently being sung about the coward who shot Jesse in the back.

So many people came to view the body of their dead hero that they had to pack the body in ice to keep it from rotting. Eventually, though, even a frozen Jesse wouldn't keep, so the family had to bury him.

It is important to note that thousands of people saw the body and no one questioned who this person had been. But after about ten or fifteen years, when many of the witnesses were gone or scattered elsewhere, loose tongues began to wag. People who didn't want to believe that Jesse was dead began to tell stories that Jesse had escaped to Canada or New Zealand or some such place, and was still alive. To make matters worse, about 1920 some old coot, on his death bed claimed that Jesse had indeed escaped, and that he was, in fact, Jesse James with an altered identity.

Handwriting experts looked at the old man's handwriting and that of Jesse James. They concluded there was no similarity between the handwriting specimens of the two men, both of whom wrote full-page letters. Also, the old man would have been 105 years old when he died, if he were Jesse James, and he wasn't.

Evidence, of course, did not stop people from believing what they wanted to believe. The old man's children began to call themselves descendants of Jesse James. It was better than being nobodies.

Of course, the real descendants of Jesse contested the claims of these new family members. Both sides took their case to a judge. They wanted permission to dig up the body of Jesse and see what they could find to support their claims. The judge agreed that not knowing who was in the grave was reason enough to open it, so he allowed an exhumation.

Four scientists volunteered to do tests, so in 1995, the grave was opened. There was a great deal of ground water, which meant that the body would be in bad shape. Sure enough, the pine box he had been buried in had rotted away. Nothing was left but a few bones and some gooey clay.

Right away, the scientists determined the bones were of a Caucasian male, about five foot ten in height, around thirty-five years old, who had been shot in the head. They also found a bullet in the mud which came from a spot where as a young man, Jesse was shot, but not injured seriously.

All these facts, however, did not prove whose bones these were. A DNA scientist went to work on the them but there wasn't a complete pattern for him to work with. Next, he took some teeth from the body. There were eighteen teeth left. Drilling into the teeth he found more bits of DNA but still not enough for a complete sample.

Next, the scientists asked to dig up the body of Jesse's mother, Zerelda James Samuell. They could not get permission to exhume her, however. A judge would allow the exhumation of a body where there was a question of identity; there was no question about the body in Zerelda's grave.

So the scientist looked for and found descendants of Jesse's sister Elizabeth. There were two men available, one much older than the other. They were not father and son, but were cousins. Of course, there were similarities in their DNA, because they had a common ancestor, Elizabeth.

Then all the scientists on the team held their breath while a comparison was made of DNA from the two men to the DNA bits that came from the teeth of the body in Jesse's grave.

There was a partial match between the DNA of the body and that of the descendants of Elizabeth. Since this would hardly ever happen by chance, the scientists determined that the body was that of a descendant of Zerelda James Samuel, and most likely, Jesse James.

And that should end the story. But it didn't. People believe what they want to believe. Now they are going to dig up the body of the old man who claimed to have been the "Real" Jesse James.

So, don't be too hard on the O. J. Simpson jurors for ignoring the DNA evidence. They are not alone in this world. As long as there are conspiracy theorists, there will be people who want to believe.

This is not the first time it has happened. People who understand science seem to be few and far between. Do you know that President Lincoln was dug up twice? He was murdered in April of 1865. Several years afterwards, word of a conspiracy got around and people were told that he didn't really die. So, he was dug up. Sure enough, the body in the casket was of a lanky man who sure looked like Lincoln, and he had been shot in the head, and all. They didn't have DNA evidence then, but the conclusion of the best scientists of the time was that it was indeed Lincoln in the coffin.

Well, the stories continued to circulate and grew quite loud by 1899. So once again, Lincoln was dug up, and once again, the results were the same: he hadn't gone anywhere and was still lying in his coffin. What was left of the body was as close to Abraham Lincoln as anyone could imagine. This time he was put in about one hundred and fifty tons of cement, so no one could dig him up ever again.

Now, people want to dig up the body of John Wilkes Booth, the man who killed Lincoln. There is a conspiracy theory about his not being the right body in the casket, as though we haven't heard that before. I guess it is something to do on a Saturday night when TV does not satisfy. Too bad people did not take time to learn some science when they were in school.

I hope you folks will be the ones who know math and science and will be the ones to recognize baloney when you hear it. After all, you will be the ones on the juries in the future. You will be the ones who vote and do all the important things in life. If any of my generation is left, they will be depending on you to do the intelligent thing for us.

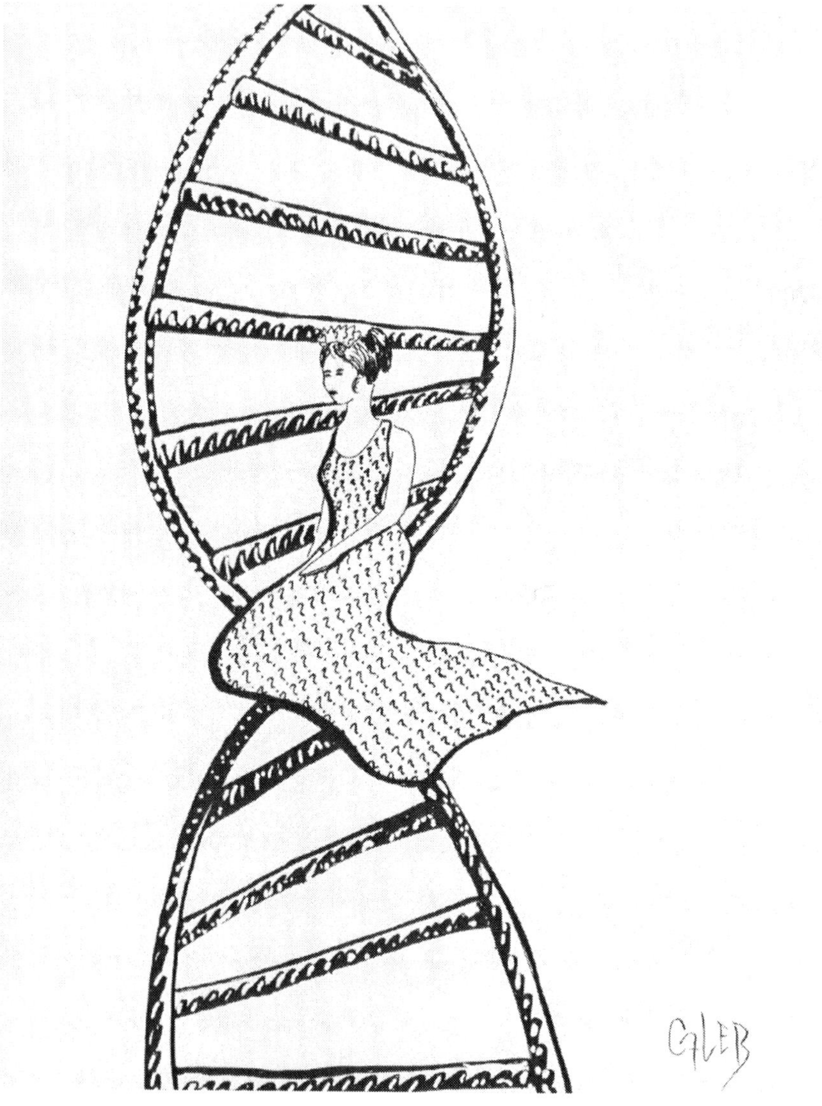

The real Anastasia, whose place in history was protected by a strand of DNA (in the background). The fake Anastasia was discovered through DNA evidence.

The Great Impostor

Once there was a Tsar (emperor) of all the Russias. He was an absolute monarch, the most powerful ruler of his time in the whole world, and he was not very kind to his people. The year was about 1916, so you can see that this story takes place some time ago. But it is very true, nonetheless.

Well, the Tsar had several children and they all lived in a fine palace. But many of his subjects were desperately poor. And they began a revolt against the Tsar and his royal family and all the nobility which had oppressed them for so long. The rest of the western world watched in horror as the revolutionaries took over. They seized the royal family but didn't quite know what to do with them. Many of the royal families in Europe were related and they didn't want to see their cousins come to a bad end.

It was the Communists who wrested power from the revolutionaries. They decided to murder the Tsar and his family and be done with them. So they took the family, I think there were five children, their mother and father, and their family physician, to a large house in Siberia. One night all the family were taken to a lower floor of the building and shot. The bullets did not act fast enough, so their heads were smashed in with rifle butts.

Bodies of the family were taken out to a wood in Siberia and buried. We know all this because when Communism failed in Russia a few years ago, a report was dug up which showed the order to kill the royal family. It was written by Lenin. Another report told what happened to the family and where they were buried.

But the story is getting ahead of itself. About 1922, a young woman was pulled from a canal in Germany. It appeared that she had tried to kill herself. She mumbled something about the Russian royal family, whose name was Romanov. And she claimed to have been a daughter of that family, who escaped the execution, named Anastasia. No one believed her and she was locked up for a year or so in an institution.

But curious people began to listen to her. She looked like Anastasia and she knew quite a bit about the Romanov family. There were Romanov cousins who were not caught up in the revolution in Russia, and they conducted an investigation. They decided she was not Anastasia, but more and more other people became convinced she was.

The Romanov family hired a detective who found a photograph of the young woman. He said in 1925 she was a daughter of a polish factory worker, not one of the Romanovs. A German court had a world-famous trial which decided that she did not prove her case, and so her claim on the Romanov fortune was denied. They had one hundred million dollars worth of assets outside of Russia.

Next, writers interviewed Anastasia and one made a play about her. The play was made into a movie. It was very dramatic as it showed how she escaped from the execution in Siberia and made her way to Germany. Of course, the movie makers did not say the woman was Anastasia, but it left plenty of room for a person to come to that conclusion. In other words, the writers believed her.

Anastasia lived a long, full life. Over the years many others in royal families made friends with her and became absolutely convinced that she was Anastasia. And I can tell you that the mystery of her life has held my attention over the years.

Well, Anastasia died a few years ago. Until the very end, she maintained that she was the daughter of the Tsar. Her will directed that she be cremated. Some said this was a deliberate effort to hide any trace of her DNA so she would forever be a mystery.

In the meantime, people found the old Russian records and set out to find the burial site of the family. And they did find their bones, except for two people: Anastasia and her little brother . The records said that two bodies were burned elsewhere and that should explain what happened. But of course, Anastasia's friends said what really happened was that Anastasia and the boy got away, but that the boy died.

To identify the bones found in Siberia, scientists asked for and got a sample of blood from Prince Philip, husband of the Queen of England. He was a close cousin of the Romanov family. Sure enough, Prince Philip's DNA matched that of the bones found in the Siberian woods.

Then scientists decided to look for a sample of DNA from Anastasia. Since she had been cremated, there wasn't any to examine. Except for one sample, that is. Ten years before, Anastasia had surgery and a sample of her tissue had been retained by doctors in her hospital. She was not aware they had done this.

Well, the DNA taken from Anastasia did not match that of Prince Philip or the bones in the Siberian woods. But there was a match for her DNA. A descendant of the Polish factory worker was found. His DNA matched the sample taken from the hospital tissue.

Thus, Anastasia's DNA was given a double test—what it did not match and what it did match. The scientific evidence was clear: Anastasia was a fraud. She was a very convincing fraud, but a fraud nonetheless. How she obtained knowledge of the Romanov family is not known to this day, but with this knowledge, she fooled many people.

Anastasia still fools some people. A writer who supported her cause said, "But you don't understand! These science tests don't take into account human experience!"

Thank heavens, they don't take human experience into account! They are not supposed to. They are supposed to ignore such subjective data and focus only on what can be measured.

An intelligent, educated writer wants to nullify the evidence so his ideas can be carried forward. We shouldn't be too hard on juries that are not so well educated and trained when they fail to understand all that modern science can tell them. We need to find ways to make science more understandable and important to them. That is just one of the reasons why schools spend so much time on science. It is important for all of us to learn to separate the real Anastasia from the false ones as we go through life.

Bill Smoot votes against "liberty and justice for all."

With Liberty and Justice for Some

Do you remember the last part of the Pledge of Allegiance to the Flag? It says, "with liberty and justice for all." I am going to tell a story about a man who believed in that phrase. He took it so seriously it cost him his life.

I first heard about it when my grandmother told me about her dad. She said she never knew him. I, of course, as small boys do, wanted to know more.

"Why didn't you know your father?" I asked.

"He died when I was a baby—about a year old," she told me.

"Why did he die?" I kept on.

"He was killed," she said.

"Who killed him?"

"I don't know," she said.

"Do you know anything else?" I responded.

"Oh, when I was about 16, we were living in a different town, about thirty miles away. It was dusk and I was going home from my girlfriend's house. I always had to be home by dark. Georgetown was almost deserted, and when I got to a large intersection, a man stepped in front of me."

"What did he look like?" I asked.

"He just a was a farmer. Shadows were long and I couldn't see him very well. He said, 'Are you Stella Walker?' I said I was and asked if we knew him. I meant if our family knew him. I was getting scared of being alone on the street with him. He said 'No, they don't know me, but I shot your father. Can you forgive me?'"

"Wow!" I said, "I bet you were frightened!"

"Yes, I surely was scared. I told the man, 'Only God can forgive,' and I ran home"

"Did you tell the sheriff?' I asked.
"Yes."
"Did you tell your mother?"
"Yes"
"Well, what did they do?" I asked in my impatient, small boy manner.
"They didn't do anything," she said, trying to recall all the details.

Well, now I know who the man was, and I know why he said what he did, and I know why he wasn't arrested.

It was 1874 and James M. Walker lived in a small town in Kentucky. The War Between the States had ended nine years before, but feelings still ran high. James lived in a Southern area, but he had served in the Union Army. Now he was a prosperous businessman with his five brothers. In their county a group formed itself from the unhappy losers of the War. It was also happening all over, in the North as well as the South. They called themselves Ku Klux Klan, and they were very unhappy that the Black people were no longer slaves.

The Klan in Walker's area had been conducting a war of terror against defenseless Black people. They were killing little boys and girls, and then their parents, if these poor people did not leave the area.

The Walkers and some other white people thought this was horrible and they were trying to stop the Klan. They wanted freedom for everyone, and they hated the idea of killing. The method they adopted to end the killing was to get the Federal government to arrest Klan members. State courts could not get anyone to be a witness against the Klan or to convict the Klan. Witnesses and jurors who did, did not live long.

Eventually a few Klansmen were taken off to jail. The local chief of the Klan was a man named Bill Smoot. He was raised next door to the Walkers and knew them well. But the Klan was a secret organization, so the Walkers did not know Smoot was in the Klan. They were pretty sure the sheriff was in the Klan, however. The Klan pretty well owned the law, the justice system, and the local newspapers.

Members of the Klan, wearing hoods, kept telling the Walkers to quit getting in their way. But the Walker brothers kept on.

Finally, on the fourth of May, a rainy Monday afternoon, Bill Smoot and his brother, John, shot James Walker in the back. They chose to do it where everyone could see them as a warning to anyone else who might get in their way. Then they took over the town and most of the county, chasing and trying to kill as many of the "good guys" as possible.

The Civil War almost started again before order was restored. But two of the Walkers were dead and others fled for their lives before it was all over. Bill Smoot went to prison.

John Smoot was killed, so the only person who could truthfully say to my grandmother, "I shot your father," was Bill Smoot. He had been released from prison by then. He didn't know what my grandmother looked like, since she was a baby when she lived near him, so he had to track her down in another city. We think he really wanted to know, "Is your family looking for me?"

We tend to take freedom for granted. We forget that freedom costs money and lives. Its cost is very high. There are always people wanting to take our freedom away from us. It might be "elite" people in government who think they know what is best for us. Or it might be a new edition of the Ku Klux Klan or another group that bases its activity on the skin color of other people, or maybe their religion. But they never go away.

Until we say, "with liberty and justice for all," and actually believe it, the problems will continue.

No telling what you'll find in an old privy pit

Genteel Art of Privy Digging

It was a hot day. Perspiration was rolling down my arms and down my back. Normally, I would be miserable and complaining but this was one of my happiest times. I was in Kentucky, far from my California home, and wandering around the farm my great-great-grandparents bought in 1881. They were Asa Grover and his wife Martha.

Asa was a lawyer and a banker. He had come to Kentucky in 1837 from western New York state. He set up a farm in another county and also became a politician. By 1865, Asa was a U.S. Congressman from the largest Kentucky district. Now he had moved to yet another county and had begun a bank in town. Life was good to Asa.

The Grovers lived in the small town of Georgetown during the week, but returned to this farm on week-ends. And I was getting an opportunity to inspect their land in every nook and cranny. My cousin owned it now, and he invited me out to see the place. So I flew from California to the middle of Kentucky just to take the tour.

The farm sported a fine barn and healthy cattle. It had gentle rolling hills that led to a deep creek called a Fork of the Elkhorn. The land was not rocky as was the land on some farms in the neighborhood.

An old house stood on the top of the highest of the small hills. It had a good view and a deep well beside it. That is where my ancestors lived out their lives in peace. All in all, it was a good Kentucky farm.

My cousin Horace was good company as we wandered from place to place. He showed me the place where the French General Lafayette came to speak to people so he could encourage young men to join in the battle for the War of 1812. Kentucky supplied many soldiers for that War.

It was an interesting day. As we were walking back to my cousin's truck to go back to town and my car, I asked a silly question: "Horace, why did Asa, a man from western New York, buy this particular farm?

He could have bought any other piece of property, but he bought this one, which was four miles from town and his business."

Horace thought a bit and speculated some, but he finally concluded that he didn't know the reason.

When I got back to California, I began to check some records. I had a great-great-great-great-grandfather, Lewis Vallandingham, who lived in that part of the country. He set up a farm in about 1786, when the Revolutionary War ended. Deeds for all those properties burned in the 1830's, so all I had to go on were references to the location from old letters. The best reference said that the farm was four miles west of Georgetown on McConnell's Run. I knew a run was a very small creek.

So I wrote Horace a letter and asked him where his farm was in relation to Georgetown. He said it was four miles west. Then I asked him if there was a creek known as McConnell's Run in the area. It took about a month, but Horace copied and glued together aerial maps of the area, showing that McConnell's Run was at the foot of his farm.

Next, I asked Horace to tell me about the farms around the area, and tell me which one was best for growing food, and which had a high point where one could see Indians coming. He surveyed all of them and said his farm met that description best.

Then I checked the records once more. I found that Asa's wife, Martha, was a granddaughter of Lewis Vallandingham! And then it struck me—*the reason Asa bought that particular farm was that his wife wanted it.* It was part of her heritage! She knew it. Her mother lived with them, and most likely her mother was married in the old house that stood on a hill and stands there today. Of course, she knew Lewis, her father-in-law, personally.

So the farm, it appeared, was not only family property from 1881, it had been in the family about a hundred years before, from around 1786 when Kentucky was Indian land, and the British were paying Indians to murder the settlers.

Who could blame me for wanting to do some digging to find old artifacts to prove my story? But with my arthritis and my cousin's arthritis, we were in no shape to dig. Do you know what we wanted to dig up? The old privy locations. It is an ancient and honorable tactic for archeologists to dig up privies, where all kinds of things can be found beside the obvious.

A privy is an outhouse, the building you used when there was no indoor plumbing, and you needed a bathroom. People threw or lost things in privvies that are waiting to be discovered many years later.

Construction was primitive. Holes were dug in the ground and lined with brick or something to keep the walls from caving in. Then wooden buildings were placed over the holes. They were wooden so they could be moved to another hole when the first one got filled up. Seldom were outhouses built of brick or stone.

After a hundred or so years (maybe three hundred years in coastal Virginia), archeologists dig into these old pits to see what they can find. They find bits of pottery, coins, guns, toys and all sorts of other junk, which tell a lot about the times of the folks who dropped them in.

Finding abandoned pits and locating artifacts is both a science and an art. Books have been written on the subject. And that is what I wanted to do on Horace's farm in Kentucky. But I have not found time and workers to do it. It is one of my goals.

It is nice to have goals in life. Science is fun.

The man washing the pig is Caleb's puzzle. In his opinion the story is Hogwash!

The Real "Man without a Country"

Believe it or not, the United States Senate in Washington has a chaplain. This is a preacher, priest, or rabbi who leads public prayers as the Senate begins its deliberation each day. There is no evidence that these prayers do the slightest bit of good, but the practice continues.

After the War Between the States, it must have been about 1865, a minister (parson), who later became the chaplain of the Senate, heard a story about a congressman who was sent away from his country. This sad tale led him to write a story about a similar person.

The good parson named the man Philip Nolan. Philip was exiled from his beloved America for some misdeed or another. He was placed on board a ship, and wherever the ship went, he was not allowed to get off. Each country the ship went to did not want the man on its shores. So the man was very sad that he had lost his wonderful country, and that no one else would have him.

The story is partially true. A man was exiled from the Union side of America about 1863. He was a Congressman from Ohio, who was bugging President Lincoln about the disastrous effects of the War Between the States. Many hundreds of thousands of American boys were being killed. But Mr. Lincoln kept on with the War and got really mad at the Congressman.

The congressman was loyal to the Union side, but he had many relatives in the South and was hoping to avoid all the bloodshed. His name in real life was Clement Laird Vallandigham. His dad was a brother of my ancestor. That is how I know so much about him.

President Lincoln had Clement arrested on a false charge of being loyal to the South. The real problem was that Vallandigham was in one political party and Lincoln was in the other. It was a case of "Politics as Usual." Presidents can't arrest congressmen or anyone else because of what they say, so President Lincoln waited until Clement lost an election. President

Lincoln then had him sent across the Southern lines.

Well, Vallandigham was no friend of the South, and the Southerners didn't know what to do with him. They probably said something like, "O.K., Bud, but would you please get out of the way? We're trying to conduct a war here."

Vallandigham worked his way to the Atlantic coast where he hitched a ride on board a ship that was headed for Canada. He went across Canada until he got to the Detroit River near the American city of Detroit. There he found many Southerners who also had to flee from the occupied territories of the South.

Vallandigham didn't sit around and cuss his bad luck as Philip Nolan did in the story. Nope, he sneaked back into Ohio and ran a campaign for Governor and almost won. He was defeated by Lincoln. Some said the President got soldiers to act as citizens of Ohio, even though they were from other states, and vote in the Ohio election. Whatever the case, there were many more votes in that election than there were voters!

Again, it was just a matter of Republicans against Democrats involving dirty politics, and had little to do with the North and South battles. Vallandigham was not really a "man without a country."

Eventually, Vallandigham was allowed back into Ohio. As soon as the War was over in 1865 and Lincoln was assassinated, Vallandigham established a very good law career. He was popular in Ohio. He died at the age of fifty-one while demonstrating at a trial how a pistol was fired. He had shot himself by mistake.

Bitter enemies, both Lincoln and Vallandigham died from wounds inflicted by a pistol.

Remember that famous story I mentioned? It was supposed to have appeared in a magazine called *The Atlantic Monthly* just before the Ohio election to embarrass Vallandigham. But it was late getting published. The good parson wrote one of the most popular stories of his time, which was still being read in literature classes until a few years ago. Then it became unpopular to be sentimental and patriotic about America. His story has since been forgotten.

I suppose that is just as well. It wasn't a true story. But real events like those that happened to Vallandigham are what make history so interesting.

Great things can come from old underwear?

Old Underwear

Five hundred years ago teachers could work with about two students, no more. They would show their students their "treasures," which would be parchment scrolls with some information on them. This was all they had to work with. And you can imagine that the only students to be educated were the children of Kings and other noble families. With them and a few church people, there were very few educated people in the world.

Certainly, the children of kings were not going to be teachers. They were too important for that. So, whatever education there was tended to stay in a small, select group.

But something came along to change all that. Suddenly a teacher could teach 20 or more students. And chances were that of those twenty students, two might go into teaching. They would each teach twenty more. The first thing you know, there was an information explosion all over the western world!

What was the invention that made it all possible? Why, the book, of course. Somebody had to invent the book. That invention made it possible and useful for people over wide areas to read.

Books began to spread knowledge, and with that knowledge came a lessening of importance of the Church and the Nobility. No one had to depend on them for information anymore. Books showed how to build a house, how to treat a wound, how to understand the Bible, and what foods to eat and to avoid. I am sure they mentioned the hazards of eating the mold on cheese and the problems with yellow snow. They showed which mushrooms were good and which were to be used on your enemies.

So the educated part of the world began to live better than ever, because people had knowledge for the first time. You thought I was going to say school books did all this, but it was not just school books that were invented.

Of course, the invention that made books possible was the printing press. And that was a marvelous device. Chinese folks had moveable type for many years but it was old Gutenberg who put it all together in a printed page. What book was the first one printed? Why, the Bible, of course.

No matter how clever Gutenberg was, he needed one more thing before he could use his printing press. Know what it was? No, he had ink. It was paper! That's right. In those days you couldn't run down to the corner drug store and buy paper for your printing press. That is because there wasn't a corner, there wasn't a drug store, and there wasn't any paper. Well, a few sheets were made for special purposes, but that is all.

Just before all these days of invention there was a plague in Europe. Some say about half the population was wiped out. And those who were left alive celebrated. They gave thanks, they gave parties, and they gave themselves something they never had before: underwear.

Many survivors had been too poor to afford underwear. But now they were wealthier because all the dead left their belongings to the living, and they could afford these garments. People took the flax plant, which was like a weed, and made linen cloth out of it. They made underwear from linen. Today some of the finest clothing in the world is made of linen.

What do you do with old underwear when you are finished with it? You throw it away, that's what. Piles of it began collecting in corners of Europe. Ragpickers wondered what to do with the stuff, there was so much of it. And then one day a man figured out what he could do that would make him lots of money.

This man, we do not know who he was, put piles of old underwear in tubs of water near a waterwheel, and rigged a hammer so it would pound the old cloth into a pulp. Then he would spread a thin layer of pulp on a flat surface and would let it dry. What he got was some of the finest paper in the world! Linen paper. It is still some of the best paper in use today. Of course, he took his paper and sold it to people who owned printing presses. Then they were able to make books, which would sell at great prices everywhere.

Think about it: You can still find original Gutenberg Bibles in existence today. You can read the wonderful Twenty-third Psalm with its grand prose, soaring thoughts and theological introspection in that Bible, and you can say, "Wow, that was printed on somebody's shorts!"

We can be sure that the second largest information explosion in the western world was made possible by old underwear.

"What?" you say, "If that was the second largest information explosion, what was the largest?"

Glad you asked. You are now living in the middle of the largest information explosion. Few people recognize that fact because we are so close to it. About thirty years ago another invention was made which changed all our lives.

That's right, it was the computer. Now, even large sets of books such as encyclopedias are stored on a CD or two. News flies from spot to spot across the world on networks in a few minutes. It used to be that-mankind's total supply of knowledge doubled every thousand years. Then books came along and it doubled every hundred years. Early computers came out and it doubled every ten years. With the latest developments in computers some say our supply of knowledge doubles every year. Where do we put it all? That is our new problem.

Some old houses are spooky, some just hold memories

Indivisible
And the Secret Staircase

When we say the pledge to the flag every morning, we say several words that are new to us. One of them is "indivisible." Do you know what it means? It means you can't divide it. Divide what? You can't divide the Country.

"Why bring that up?" you ask. Good question. There is a need to remind ourselves, because at one time people tried to divide the Country. My folks tried it. They were Southerners, and in 1861 they went to war to separate themselves from the Northern States. They wanted to set up their own country and just be left alone. But I am getting ahead of my story.

It had taken me forty years to get back to a small county in Kentucky, but I finally did it. I wanted to see an old house where my great grandfather lived. I had heard a lot about it, you see, and wanted to have a look before I died. He was a Judge for many years so I am going to call him Judge Pryor.

Since I lived in California, it seemed that I might never get the opportunity. Henry County, Kentucky, was 2000 miles away. But one day, I just said, "Nuts. I have a few days to myself. I believe I'll go."

So I called my brother, who lived about eighty miles from the old place and asked if he would go with me. He had been quite sick and was unable to travel, but he said, "Nuts. I've seen everything around here. I believe I'll go."

I flew to Kentucky, rented a car and got my brother. We drove the eighty miles to New Castle in about an hour and a half. We found a cousin who lived near the old house, and he called the present owner to ask if we could see it. He explained that my brother and I were great-grandchildren of the man who built the house one hundred thirty-five years ago.

The owners were delighted to have us look at the place. In a few minutes we went three miles up a country road to a large old brick house. It was in perfect shape. My mother had told me the bricks were made right there on the property. It was her grandfather's home, and she spent many happy days living there.

We discovered from the owners that my grandfather, a son of the man who built the place, owned it for many years, and when he died, he left it to his wife, my grandmother. She sold it in the 1930's. The people who bought the place kept it for about twenty years and then sold it to the present owners. They were the ones who put it in new condition, and who stocked it full of wonderful old antiques.

The tour began. We saw twelve foot high ceilings in spacious rooms with artistic plaster moldings that were installed in 1859. The formal dining room was large. Old newspapers said Judge Pryor held many dinner parties there, inviting some of the most famous people of his time. There was a wonderful staircase leading upstairs. It had a cherry railing. The floors up there were made of wide, pine boards. Trees don't exist these days that would provide such fine lumber. The boards were wonderfully mellow with the color of over a hundred years of use.

Memories lingered in every corner, caught in the reflections of the sun on cut glass vases and in the cobwebs of very old spiders.

My brother and I took pictures as we roamed from room to room. Then we went upstairs, and a fun trip turned into at trip of mystery.

At the top of the stairs we visited several bedrooms. At one point we looked into a rather dark one. My brother's eyesight had been poor for years. He looked around, blinked, and said, "This is the room with the secret staircase."

It was the first time I ever heard about it. The owner was startled. He said, "Why, yes it is."

My brother said, "It was behind a closet. Where is the closet?"

The owner said in a strained voice, "It was over there." He pointed across the room toward a window. "We took it out to make room for the window. You can see where we moved some of the floor boards."

Sure enough, there were faint traces where there had been some disturbances in the flooring by the window. My brother nodded and we toured the rest of the house. But after that experience no one said much of anything.

Since I had never heard of the secret staircase, I wondered how my brother knew about it. There was no opportunity to ask him because the owner began telling a story. It turned out he knew part and I knew part and together we knew the whole thing.

The owner boasted how, during the Civil War, Confederate General

John Hunt Morgan escaped from the Yankees in Ohio. He made a bee line for this house, where he knew he would find safety. For some reason he knew Judge Pryor was a Southern sympathizer. The house was four years old then. It was late in 1863.

Morgan and his officer, a man named Hines, were welcomed and allowed to sleep late the next morning. Then Judge Pryor helped them take four of his cattle and drive them to a Southern destination where they could cross the battle lines. No one would bother them because they would look like farmers heading for a market.

The story is that the two Confederate officers slipped down the secret staircase to the outside in back of the house and were on their way.

That was the owner's story. Mine was that in the late part of 1863 Judge Pryor had been arrested by the Union Army for some reason and had been sent to prison. Now I knew why. The Yankees arrested him for helping the General escape.

Well, Judge Pryor had an uncle who knew President Lincoln personally. And Judge Pryor's niece was married to a Lincoln nephew. Someone in the Lincoln collection of family or friends asked Lincoln to let Judge Pryor go home occasionally on leave to take care of his law business and farm. And he did. But on week days, Judge Pryor always had to go back to prison.

By this time, it was about six months later, General Morgan had put together another army and was giving the Union army a very had time. General Morgan was a good general.

People in the North were getting angry that Morgan escaped and was causing them so much trouble. Their anger turned to Judge Pryor, who had helped Morgan. On one of his times off from prison, a friend told Judge Pryor that he would come to great harm the next time he went back to prison.

When Union soldiers came to take my great grandfather back to prison, his servants delayed them while he escaped out the back way through the secret staircase and fled across the Ohio River. He went on into Indiana and worked his way up to Detroit, then across the river and into Canada. He was there for a few months, then sent for his wife and children. They stayed in Amherstburg, Ontario, Canada, with many other Southerners from Kentucky until the War was over and President Lincoln was killed. They returned the following year in 1866.

Before Judge Pryor could become a practicing lawyer and farmer, he had to take a new pledge saying he would not try to separate the Union anymore. That has become a general statement and is included in our pledge to the Flag.

Immediately, Judge Pryor was appointed a circuit judge. After three years he, who had served time in prison, was appointed the chief justice of the state supreme court. He stayed on the supreme court for twenty-five years, often as the chief justice, and became one of the most famous Judges Kentucky has ever had.

Judge Pryor died in the house in 1914. He was eighty-nine years old.

Our tour was about over. My brother was getting ill, so we started back the eighty miles to his home. I still wanted to ask him about the secret staircase. While he rested, I tried once. I said, "You must have a long memory to remember that staircase."

He was tired, but he said, "Oh, I have never seen it. Mom told me about it."

The next question was, "Well, how did you know that was the right room?" But he was asleep. I flew back to California with no answer. But I wrote him a letter and asked how he knew. He didn't answer. Maybe he got caught in one of those reflections. Or maybe he was more closely tuned to the memories of the place that flitted like dust from room to room.

Eventually I called him and asked the question that had haunted me for months. He said, "I don't know how I knew. I just did."

And we still do not know why Judge Pryor built that staircase, but we know why that word "indivisible" is in the pledge to the Flag.

Imagined tombstone for Henry Bruce Vallandingham

Expensive Words

Hiring people to do your dirty work is nothing new in this country. I am sure the practice came here with the early settlers. Certainly the French and British paid Indians to kill those Europeans who dared to leave the area around the Atlantic ocean and push into the interior of the Country.

I knew that my third great-grandfather had died quite early. His first name was Henry. His tombstone said he died in 1858, and that meant he was only fifty-one years old when he went to meet his maker. It seemed young to me because I knew his parents lived to be in their eighties, and I knew he had good genes.

One day I got an email message from a distant cousin that said he had come across an old newspaper article. The article said a man with a name like my third great-grandfather's was murdered about July 18, 1856. That date sure sounded familiar. And he was murdered in Missouri, which is where Henry died.

I checked my records and found that the month and day were right, but my ancestor died two years later. I felt silly, almost jumping to the conclusion that Henry had been murdered. After all, I had a letter Henry wrote in 1856, and in that letter he said he was in a place called Feninton, Missouri. The man who was murdered lived in Lexington, Missouri.

Just to be sure, I wrote a lot of historical museums and libraries in Missouri about the location of Fenington. Every one of them wrote back that there never was and never had been a Fenington, Missouri. I looked very hard at the handwritten letter from my ancestor. And then I asked my wife, who had never seen the document before. She said the location could easily be Lexington and not Fenington. Part of the L was missing and it looked like an F to me. The first n was different from the second n, and could easily be an x. It sure was puzzling.

About that time my distant cousin sent me a copy of the old newspaper article. The last name of the victim wasn't *like* that of my ancestor, it *was* my ancestor's name. But it didn't give his first name. And the article was quite explicit.

It was clear that the man who wrote the article didn't like murdered man. I thought it odd that he used both names of the killer, but only the last name of the victim. And then I realized that newspapers used to do this when a person was of a low social status.

The article said the killer was a man named Frederick Myers, and that he ambushed the victim. He blew his stomach away with a shotgun. Then he let him bleed to death in the street. Further, he shot the victim at noon on Friday on a busy boulevard, where everyone could see him. The man calmly walked to the office of the sheriff and turned himself in. That afternoon, the local justice of the peace let Myers go, saying he was justified in his murder as a crime of passion and as self-defense.

The newspaper said self-defense was a poor defense, indicating that Henry had no weapon. And it said passion was no good as a defense, because the killer waited too many months to shoot. In fact, it said there really wasn't much sense in letting Myers go free. The whole story began to smell. I was glad that my ancestor died two years later, and wasn't involved in any of this.

If a man is going to murder someone else, he usually does it under cover of darkness. That way, no one can see what happened and ask embarrassing questions. Also, that way the victim can't easily shoot back. Suddenly some things began to fall into place. You kill people on a busy street corner at noon to let people know what you did, not to hide it. Sometimes these killings are a warning to others.

I wondered what the victim could have done that would have made others so mad at him. So my cousin and I decided to dig into the matter. We asked for court records of anyone who died on that date with the last name we had found from the article: Vallandingham.

Eventually we got the record. The man who died was Henry Vallandingham! *It was my ancestor*. But that meant the tombstone was wrong!

Then I remembered some notes I had. Henry was buried in Kentucky where I took a photo of his tombstone, but he died in Missouri! His body was dug up about 1887, and moved to Kentucky, thirty-one years after he died. And he got a new tombstone. It was probably done from memory and his wife got the date wrong.

No wonder historians have hard lives. About the only thing written in stone you can believe is the Ten Commandments. It surely isn't tombstones.

So now I really got interested in what was going on in Lexington, Missouri, in 1856. And I found out.

Lexington was close to the Kansas Territory. Kansas was about to enter the Union as a new state. The question was, should it enter the Union as a free state or a slave state? Slavery was quite legal. But people were divided over whether slavery should be expanded. The Northern part of the country said, NO! The South said YES! And Lexington, Missouri, was full of pro-slavery people, determined that their neighbor would become a slave state.

When Kansas became a state, it would get two senators and several congressmen. These people would vote in Congress the way the state went. If Kansas were to become slave, these officials would vote for slavery in the Congress. If Kansas were to vote for freedom, those senators and congressmen would vote against slavery in Congress.

Well, it was such an important question that people were shooting each other over the answer. I found that the unofficial penalty for helping slaves escape from their masters was, you guessed it, death. Since all the people who were involved with the killer, Myers, were pro-slavery, plus other evidence, it became quite likely that Henry Vallandingham was helping free slaves.

I got copies of newspapers from Lexington, Missouri, in the year 1856. It was a pro-slavery newspaper. Why would a newspaper writer think Henry was such a bad guy and so low on the social scale? Perhaps it was because Henry was an abolitionist, the kind of person who wanted Kansas to enter the Union as a free state. It was doubly bad for Henry because he was also a Southerner.

And that is the way the evidence is pointing now. Myers fled the area, rather than face a grand jury indictment. Kansas only became a state, a free one, when the senators from southern states marched out of the Senate and formed their own government. That was the beginning of the War Between the States. Some call it the Civil War.

And every time I think about Henry's story, I recall how expensive freedom really is. It costs lives, and the fight for freedom is never over.

PART THREE

ODD BALL
Science and Math

A piece of amber used as a woman's pendant, containing a variety of unusual artifacts

Possibility of a Real Jurassic Park

Do you remember the movie *Jurassic Park*? Nearly everyone saw it. Now do you remember how the scientists found enough DNA to make a dinosaur? That's right, they found that mosquitoes had sucked blood from the animals, over sixty-five million years ago. But that is not all.

Do you recall how the scientists found sixty-five million year-old mosquitoes? After all, the ones that bite me are rather young. Yes, the scientists found the mosquitoes frozen in amber, the sap of trees. It hardens over time and is almost like a rock. They can polish the amber, see inside it, and find mosquitoes.

Well, in a 1995 issue of our newspaper, I see scientists have found more than mosquitoes in amber. They have found bees. The scientists cut open this amber, too. Then they took out the bees. This amber was associated with rocks that were only twenty-five million years old.

When the scientists took out the bees, they took them apart and looked into their stomachs. There they found some spore cases of bacteria that had entered the bees twenty-five million years and a few days ago.

Bacteria will form hard cases around themselves when they go through dry periods. These are called spore cases.

Scientists bathed the spore cases in nutrients to see if the bacteria would live again. The oldest known bacteria that lived were seventy years old. Also, archeologists once took lotus seeds from the tomb of a dead Egyptian. I think he had been dead some three thousand years. They soaked these lotus plant seeds for a few days and actually grew lotus plants from them! It seems some forms of life can stay dormant for a long time.

Well, the bacteria from the bees actually grew! Other scientists said this wasn't so, that bacteria from the air grew in the cultures, but our bee people said they were careful to prevent this from happening, and the twenty-five million year-old bacteria actually came back to life.

That's amazing! But do you know what these scientists did with the bacteria? You and I would probably never have thought of such a thing.

The scientists tested the bacteria to see if they produce any useful antibiotics or other medicinal compounds! You know that penicillin comes from bacteria. Well, we need better and more powerful types of penicillin these days. Scientists are now trying to find these through the ancient bacteria. Test results have not been given out yet.

Maybe, then, *Jurassic Park* isn't totally a dream. Perhaps scientists could get a whole strand of DNA from several different types of dinosaurs. They have partial sets now, but not enough to make a complete animal. It is like having a page from a book and trying to re-construct the book from that one page.

Perhaps one day scientists will find more bacteria and DNA, and who knows what else from amber. Maybe then they will be able to reproduce clones of our ancestors, too. Maybe a copy of our hundred and twenty-fifth great-grandfather or grandmother can help us understand why we dislike turnips and prefer Big Macs.

Science is truly wonderful.

Canadian native with a Canadian diamond in his hand

Diamonds in the Classroom

When we think of diamond mines, we usually think of some remote area in Africa where natives sullenly dig holes in the ground in front of big guards who carry guns. The weather is beastly hot.

It turns out that this is an incomplete picture. Not only are the modern workers represented by unions, but also they have limited working hours. And Africa is not the only place where diamonds can be found. Nowadays, Eskimos have joined the search. Far from the heat of the African desert, Eskimos have been recruited to find diamonds in a land where heat is only a problem when the stove goes off.

It all started with geologists trying to figure out the paths of big glaciers. These huge ice slabs, sometimes a mile and a half thick, came from the Arctic circle in Canada and slid all the way South into the States of Indiana, Illinois, Ohio and Pennsylvania. There they left rich soil which today's smart farmers used to produce great crops each year. The glaciers also left piles of rocks wherever they stopped.

You have to remember that the glaciers advanced, scouring the Earth, then retreated all the way back to the Arctic Circle. As they melted and retreated, they created lakes and left piles of rocks.

Glacier rock piles look different from other rock piles because their rocks are large and medium-sized and small, all piled together. Regular rock piles are usually graduated into distinct sizes. They are often caused by flowing water, so that smallest rocks are carried the farthest, medium sized rocks are carried almost as far, and large rocks seldom travel at all.

Also, glacial rock piles consist of a strange collection of rocks, rocks that don't belong with each other or with the territory in which you find them. If rocks washed down from a mountain, they would generally be the same size and type as those still in the mountain. But if a glacier brought them from different places, they would not be like each other or like the surrounding rocks.

To make matters more confusing, some of the piles of rocks that came out of Canada had diamonds in them. That's right, Diamonds.

The presence of diamonds in glacial rock piles meant that somewhere along the way, glaciers scraped across places where diamonds had been made in the Earth's crust.

Diamonds are formed under intense heat and pressure. These are normally the conditions present when volcanic tubes erupt and pour hot lava out of the bowels of the Earth. Often for diamonds to form, the lava tubes appear in the presence of an unusual blue clay.

Some of you know that companies such as General Electric make diamonds. They place carbon in a mass of blue clay and then put the mixture under intense heat and pressure for a few hours. Then they knock off the blue clay and find that the carbon has been converted into a real diamond. It is a long, expensive process, but it is cheaper than the price of natural diamonds.

It was about 1965 when I first heard about the diamonds in rock piles left by glaciers. My geology professor told our class about them. Some enterprising geologists plotted the locations of the diamond finds across the United States and Canada. Then they drew lines through the sites. Sure enough, the lines pointed north, showing the direction from where the glaciers came.

Interestingly enough, the lines converged in one spot in the far north. It was in this area where the diamond tubes might be.

As luck would have it, the area was quite large, and it seemed to be covered with deep snow and ice almost all year long. People made a few sporadic trips to this large remote area, but found no clues about the location of the volcanic tubes. The area contained some of the oldest rocks on the face of the Earth, some even showing impact craters from meteors that had hit the Earth a million or so years in the past. But no diamonds. For the next twenty-five years the tubes remained hidden.

Then, about 1991, I read in newspapers that diamonds had been discovered in Canada. People were startled and amazed. Who ever heard of diamonds in Canada? I did, and I thought about my geology professor in Cleveland, Ohio, whose eyes lit up when he told us about the mysterious diamonds in the far north. I wonder if he were the one who found them.

Any of us could have gone north to locate them. The research papers were available for all to see. And someone finally did and struck it rich. You never know where the diamonds are going to be found in your science classes, do you?

Perhaps a small gene pool where inherited problems are multiplied, led to the famous "Jack the Ripper" murders

A Strange Kind of Pool

When we think about the industrial revolution, we generally think about machines, factories, and dirty air. And this is somewhat true, making a huge difference in the way people lived in the western world.

Actually, the industrial revolution came about partially as a result of two related conditions. One was thirty years of almost perfect weather that occurred in the early 1700's. Generally, people (except the few rich) had to spend all their time looking for food and some way to stay warm. They had no time to sit around and think of inventions or new religions. For the first time in modern history, good weather led to a huge supply of food and good living conditions that allowed many people time to sit back and think.

The second condition that furthered the industrial revolution was religious upheaval. Some people began to revolt against the established churches. In England, they were banished from most activities in standard English social life. But they were not banished from commerce. And that is where they excelled. James Watt, the inventor of the steam engine, was one of these social outcasts because of his religious affiliation.

It was the religious reformers who kept the industrial revolution spreading with their adherence to hard work, temperance, piousness, and self-reliance. In other words, they had family values.

As the industrial revolution took over England and spread through Europe and into America, something unusual began to happen to people. Before the Industrial revolution, people often married someone within seven miles of their homes. This was because transportation was very poor, and there was not much reason to go more than seven miles anyway, because there wasn't much to see.

As you might guess, families became heavily intermixed because it was difficult to find a wife who was not some kind of cousin, (as long as a man's choices were kept to all the available girls in a small area.)

Constant marrying of cousins led to combinations of genes in people that were repeated often. This led in turn to some rather eccentric people, a few crazy ones, and sometimes some very sick ones. On the whole, people did fairly well, but not as well as they would have done if new genes had been introduced into the "pool" of genes available.

Royalty has the same problem even today. The royal families of Europe are heavily inbred. After all, who is good enough to be in a royal family except other royal people? World War One was really a family squabble, since the heads of many of the warring nations were descendants of Queen Victoria of England. They were close cousins. Victoria transmitted a dread disease to which several male children succumbed. It was hemophilia, a genetic disorder in which one cannot stop bleeding.

It is often thought that Jack the Ripper was really the Duke of Clarence, a royal prince who was completely crazy, but who got free from time to time. When he escaped, the story goes, he would immediately go to the poor section of London and carve up young women. Whatever else the Duke was, he was reported to be less than sane. Perhaps this was due to inbreeding, in which weak genes were duplicated in his makeup.

What the industrial revolution did for many people except the Royal family, was to increase the human gene pool into a gene *lake.* In other words, as transportation became available, people began to marry outside their seven mile circle and people became genetically healthier. But the best is yet to come.

In America, the new land where there was even more freedom, people who were sturdy adventurers, both men and women, came thousands of miles from all over the western world. They married and produced children from genes that were very different, and something wonderful happened.

There is a biological concept called Hybrid Vigor. It refers to the fact that when two very different sets of genes from the same species are mixed, the resulting offspring may have more strength, resistance to disease, and better everything else. In the case of people, hybrid vigor may also mean more brains, energy, and inventiveness, as well as more strength and increased size.

That sort of thing may have happened in America as people from, say, Germany, met and married people from Norway or England or Spain or France. In America, the gene pool had become first a gene lake and then a gene ocean. The American society became a robust group of people. They thought they could solve any problem. And they carried the industrial revolution much farther than the folks did in England and Europe.

The really neat thing is that people are still coming. Some of you are children of parents from some "old country." Your parents didn't come here in old wooden boats, they came here in Boeing 747 airplanes.

Even the children and grandchildren of American slaves have made big contributions to American society. For instance, it was an African-American who invented the process for getting gasoline out of oil, so we could drive our cars. There were many more contributions, too many to name.

The key is that every group who comes here brings something and contributes something.

And we owe it all to thirty years of good weather. Those opportunities don't come to every generation. We have to take advantage of each opportunity by being ready, by being educated, and by being willing to take risks.

The DA tells a jury about alcohol intake

Death, Math, and the Average Citizen

This is a sad story. It involves the trial of a man who killed two young people, so it is important. People love to hear about trials, don't they? So, here goes:

I had a daughter. People always say, "That is a strange remark." But it is true. Several years ago I had a pretty stepdaughter named Julie. She and Kevin, her fiancée were going to get married and live happily ever after. Julie had graduated from college and was considering going on to law school. She was very bright.

One day Julie and Kevin went to see some friends. Afterwards, Kevin was taking Julie home down a freeway, which had only three cars on it. Unfortunately for them, that was one car too many.

They were happy, sober, and tired from a long day. And they were observing the speed limit, a witness said. A drunk driver was speeding down the freeway in the same direction as Julie and Kevin. He came up behind them at a very fast rate and saw he was going to hit them, so he pulled his car to the left. He almost made it.

Hit hard on the left rear, their car suddenly made a right turn. It slid off the freeway and piled into a stand of trees.

Kevin was driving. He was crushed and died almost immediately. Julie was thrown all over the car. She had many fractures but was alive, and unconscious. Police came and took her to a nearby emergency hospital. We sat with her for four days until she died. She never regained consciousness.

A big man driving a pickup truck saw the accident and forced the drunk driver off the road. Then he made the drunken young man wait until police came. The police arrested the killer and put him in jail.

Those of us in Julie's and Kevin's family went to two funerals. Then we went through a long sad period, asking ourselves, "Why?" We exchanged photographs of the dead couple and did all the things people do when they lose a loved one.

But there was one more thing to do. Several months later we had to go to the trial of the drunk driver and hear all about it one more time. The DA (District Attorney) asked us to show the jury that some one cared about Julie and Kevin. So we went. And this is what makes an ordinary sad story into a math story.

Four charges were placed against Oscar the drunk driver: drunk driving, fleeing the scene of an accident, and vehicular homicide with gross negligence, two times.

The seriousness of the case against Oscar hung on the words, "Gross Negligence." This meant he was doing something extraordinarily stupid when he killed Julie and Kevin. It was important to the defense lawyer to convince the jury that Oscar wasn't drunk at all, or at least not *very* drunk.

Oscar didn't have any money but he had a very good lawyer. The district attorney, who represents you and me in these matters, was much less experienced than the defense lawyer. But, he was persistent.

The defense lawyer said straight out, "My client wasn't drunk." This was about as big a lie as I have ever heard, according to facts we got later.

The district attorney called Oscar's wife to the witness chair and made her answer his questions. She didn't want to answer, because whatever she said would help convict her husband.

The DA asked, "Did you have a cookout the night all this happened?

"Yes."

"And did you have something to drink?"

"Yes."

"Did the drinks have alcohol in them?"

"Yes."

"What were the drinks?"

"Beer."

"How much did you have?"

"We had a six pack." The DA wrote a six on an easel he had in front of the jury.

"Did you drink it all?"

"Yes."

"Did you get more beer?"

"Yes."

"How much more beer?"

"Another six pack."

The D.A. wrote another six on the easel and continued the questioning until he had written the number twenty-four. Then he asked who drank the beer. He never mentioned Oscar. It appeared that others at the cookout drank about six beers. The DA wrote a minus six under the twenty-four. Then he asked if all the beer were gone at the end of the party, which was right before Oscar got mad and took off down the freeway to hit Julie and Kevin. Well, it turned out the beer was all gone and it was obvious that Oscar had drunk at least eighteen beers; he was *extremely* drunk.

I hadn't paid much attention to the jury. After all, they were an ordinary collection of typical Southern Californians—men and women who were Hispanic, Asian, African-American and Caucasian. They were middle-aged and older.

Then it hit me. I looked ahead at the progress of the trial and imagined it was going to include lots of math! How long had it been since these middle-aged people attended school? Did they remember any math? It is hard to find these things out when a jury is selected for a drunk driving trial. There are too many other questions to ask.

The district attorney called an expert witness to the stand. He testified that the legal definition of drunkenness was point eleven per cent alcohol in a person's blood (0.11%). It is now less than that.

Another witness said he had done a blood alcohol test on Oscar and had found that Oscar's blood alcohol content was point twenty-one per cent (0.21%). I wondered if the jury members could divide one decimal number into another and could see that Oscar was about two times the legal limit for drunkenness? The defense lawyer's statement rang in my ears: "My client wasn't drunk!"

The DA wasn't through, yet. Another expert witness said that the human body uses up alcohol at a rate such that one drink disappeared after about eight hours. He produced a graph showing usage for an average individual. The DA said, "If that is the case, then Oscar had used up some of the alcohol in his body before he was tested." The expert said that was most likely.

Reviewing information from an earlier expert, the district attorney said Oscar was tested two hours *after* the crash. The witness pointed to his graph and said Oscar's blood probably was at the point 27 per cent (0.27%) level when he hit Julie's car.

But the DA kept on. Oscar said he had been on the road for a half an hour before the incident. That meant, according to the graph, an average drinker would have had even more alcohol in his blood, because he used up some of it during the half-hour.

Oscar, it turned out, was extremely drunk when he got into his car. The statement, "My client wasn't drunk!" rang even louder. I wondered how a professional man could say such a thing.

I also wondered if the jury had understood all the math the witnesses were talking about. These were nice people who had not been to school in years.

The district attorney called one more witness. It was a teacher from a drunk driving school, who testified that Oscar was attending his classes and appeared to be learning a lot. Why was Oscar in the school? *Well, he was on probation for drunk driving when he killed Julie and Kevin.*

In an earlier crash, Oscar was drunk when he hit another car and turned his car over. He was arrested, and some lenient judge believed Oscar when he said he wouldn't do it again. The judge let Oscar go out and drive. I would like to talk with that judge! Most of us know that drunks will say anything just so we will let them continue their lives of drunkenness. Oscar had all the earmarks of a total alcoholic.

Well, I worried a lot about that jury. When the evidence was all in, the judge talked to them for an hour, telling them what they could consider and could not consider when they decided Oscar's fate. They were out of the courtroom for only fifteen minutes.

The verdict was, "GUILTY ON ALL COUNTS."

Evidently, there were enough people on the jury who understood the math of the case, and they convinced the others that Oscar was guilty.

Julie's and Kevin's families were pleased with the verdict but not the sentence. They did not want to hang Oscar. That would not bring back their kids. They were worried about *other* kids that Oscar would hit if he weren't taken off the road.

Oscar was sentenced to ten years. In California that means five years or less. The sentencing is made long to make the judges look tough. But the actual sentence is cut short. The judge apologized and said ten years was all he could do.

Julie and Kevin died ten years ago. That means Oscar has been out of prison for some time and is probably drinking and driving again.

If you haven't already guessed, I will tell you that these days it takes a lot of math to keep Society moving forward. An ignorant Society will fall apart, and there will be much extra pain if we as Lawyers, District Attorneys, Judges, Police officers and, yes, Jurors, don't know our math. You might be any of these people in the future whether you are a man or a woman. My generation has done a poor job at keeping drunks off the road. Maybe *your* generation will do better. We must keep our roads safe. It will take ordinary citizens with some understanding of math to do the job.

Chances are that a dead infant will be a boy, rather than a girl

Why Girls Are Stronger Than Boys

It is always a touchy subject to bring up—that girls are stronger than boys. But it is true, and if we are real scientists we will rely on the facts.

To get to my evidence, I need to recall a fact for you. It is this: Nature always provides more births of Male children than Female children. Is this because Males are weaker? There is no evidence for this. But there is evidence that the births run this way, roughly: forty-nine per cent girls and fifty-one per cent boys.

How can one explain this ratio of births? Scientists have tried for many years. One possible explanation is that males die sooner than females, so Nature has to provide more males to keep up with the number of females.

Let's change subjects for a moment. That ratio of forty-nine to fifty one per cent is fairly universal. If it does not exist in a large population, someone is doing something to defeat Nature.

Let me cite an example. Anthropologists were working with a tribe of Inuits around the Arctic Circle. When they began to check numbers of children, they were surprised and puzzled. There were far too many boys in the tribe for the number of girls. Knowing that the ratio of boys to girls should follow the standard pattern, they began to investigate.

The scientists made a gruesome discovery. They found that one out of five girl babies, or twenty per cent, was put out in the ice and snow to die. The tribe spokesman said it was because girls and women could not hunt. There would be too many mouths to feed if they let the girl babies live.

Whatever you think about the morality of their actions, the ratio was disturbed. That is why it was not forty-nine to fifty-one per cent.

Knowing all this, one day I found myself re-writing an old book. It was a family history on of part of my mother's family. And I found myself looking at the histories of one hundred and fourteen children born during the years 1800 to 1900.

I was looking for some diseases that might be traveling through my family line. I didn't find any diseases, but I began to make an analysis of this small population. I wanted to see if it were true that boys didn't last as long as girls.

Here is what I found at the first glance: there were fifty-seven boys born during this time and fifty-seven girls. That is almost the right ratio. My population was small, which could allow the ratio to be fifty-fifty.

Next, I looked at the children between the ages of zero years to twenty-seven years. I found that twenty-one boys died and eleven girls died. That is, about twice as many boys died as girls.

Also obvious was that twenty-eight per cent of all children died. This was possibly quite common for the times. A family had many children, knowing that it would lose nearly a fourth of them.

A magazine article recently told how a family of that time would take care of a child, but would not invest much of its emotions in the baby. That is, they would not get too close to a child for several years because the child might die, and they would be too distressed.

Now, you might wonder about the time span I chose, 28 years. It is possible for girls to die in childbirth, or for boys to get killed in a war. I was concerned about that, too, so I made another analysis. I looked into the deaths of children between the ages of zero years to ten years.

After all, during the hundred years I checked, there were several battles and wars. The worst one was the War Between the States in 1861-65. Boys could join the army if they were fourteen. So I chose ten years as a limit. That way, war would not be much of a factor unless a Southern boy of eight walked in front of a Yankee cannon.

Here is what I found: eighteen children died between the ages of zero years and ten years. Twelve of these dead children were males and six of these dead children were females. In both sets of data, boys died twice as often as girls.

I made one more check. I found that on the average boys died at the age of two years and two months, and girls died at the age of four years and six months.

Twice as many boys died as girls, and the boys died at a much earlier age.

So in this small sample, I showed that boys were more susceptible to childhood diseases and whatever else afflicted children in their first ten years.

Does this study prove that boys are weaker than girls? Only in the family studied. But the study does not disprove the theory that girls are made of sterner stuff than boys. I like to think my small study supports the theory.

Oh, and there is one more fact worth considering. In this country where insurance records are pretty good and where insurance companies make lots of money by being right, women are shown to live eight years longer, on the average, than men. So, if a man has a life expectancy of seventy-five years, a woman will have a life expectancy of eighty-three years.

So there you have it. Women seem to be made of much sterner stuff than men. The data suggest that girls are really stronger than boys.

I guess that means, boys, that since we are weaker and die off sooner, girls should take better care of us while we are here. What do you think?

Whatever you think, you can make your own analyses if you are handy with math. Math is the foundation course for all the sciences.

A surveyor looks toward trees and beyond them, Lake Erie, as he lays out Euclid Avenue in Cleveland, Ohio.

The Missing Lake

Take a look sometime at a map of the northern area of the United States from the Mississippi River all the way to New York State. This whole area is dominated by the five Great Lakes: Huron, Ontario, Michigan, Erie and Superior. But did you know they were all one big lake some fifteen thousand years ago? It is called Lake Whittlesey, even though it is now gone.

Before that time, the entire area was covered with huge glaciers, some two miles thick. That's a lot of weight. It pushed the entire central-to-northeast land-mass deep into the Earth.

When the air warmed and ice began to melt, the glaciers disappeared into fresh water. A huge lake formed in the depression left by the two mile thick mound of ice. Water from this lake poured out a river where Chicago is today. There are traces of this river still around. The water went on to the Mississippi River and worked its way to the Gulf of Mexico. There was no Niagara Falls.

Over time, the entire land mass tilted away from the Chicago area and toward the New York area. Water began to empty out of what is now Niagara Falls. As the land rose back to its original position before the heavy glaciers were on it, the level of the water dropped until the one enormous lake was gone and the five Great Lakes remained.

How can we tell there was one huge lake? It is simple. That lake left big traces of itself. One of them is called Euclid Avenue in Cleveland, Ohio. It is one of the longest avenues in the world.

You have seen a shore line, where waves come in and gently wash the sand away and leave a very flat space. Well, that is what the original big lake did. You can trace the flat shoreline all the way through Cleveland over to Chicago and up into Canada and almost all the way back to Cleveland. It is there for all to see.

Of course, every one will not recognize the old shore line. That is because smart highway engineers paved it over, and made a road out of it. In Cleveland, it is Euclid Avenue. There is even a second "bench" cut into Cleveland's hillside by the original lake. That was when the lake was even at a higher level for a long time. That area is called Terrace Drive. It was paved over, too.

Well, why not take advantage of a long, straight, flat section of land that is a gift of Nature?

Of course, the level of the land is still rising. Water is continuing to pour out of the area at Niagara Falls at a great rate. It may be that before the next ice age, the Great Lakes will be a series of little ponds. But the water has already contributed to mankind by leaving all those potential streets, so I guess it is all right to run out on us. (As if we could stop it.)

All around us there are tales of great and dramatic events in our Earth's history. It is fun to be able to notice even a few of them.

A patronizing woman tells a girl she is unique and the young lady hauls out her calculator to second the motion.

You Are Truly Unique

Do you hate it when someone tells you that you are special because you are truly unique, and you know that you are just one more kid in blue jeans?

These people are talking philosophically. But there is a mathematical process that tends to support them in a scientific way, although they never thought about it.

It begins with a famous astronomer, who wrote in one of his books about DNA. It is not a subject in his field, but about which he had become curious. He noticed the statement that one section of a DNA molecule contains roughly three hundred and twenty million (320,000,000) bits of information about the person from which it was taken. Astronomers deal in large numbers, and this may have been what caught his attention.

He wrote that "bits" was a term computer people use. He thought further that it would be wonderful if DNA bits could be converted into computer language. After all, this is the information that determines all out physical properties—sex, hair color, size of liver, height, and so on. It does not determine the choices we make, however. These occur as we grow, and nearly all of these are not pre-determined.

The astronomer knew that a computer uses eight bits to create a letter in the English language. So, an "A" takes eight bits, a "B" takes eight other bits, and so on. He divided three hundred and twenty million by eight to see how many letters our DNA could possibly contain. The answer was, of course, forty million. That's a lot of letters.

Knowing that the average English word contains five letters, he divided again. This meant that if DNA bits could be converted into English words, there would be forty divided by five, or eight million words.

A page in a book contains about two hundred fifty words. That means there would be eight million divided by two hundred fifty, or thirty-two thousand pages of information about us in one DNA molecule. With about two hundred fifty pages per book, there would be one hundred twenty-eight books about us in a DNA molecule. Wow!

Now, let's change subjects for a minute. If you roll a die, what is the possibility of coming up with a six? Yes, the answer is one in six.

What are the odds that if you roll a pair of dice that you will roll two sixes? Well, the answer is one in six times one in six, or one in thirty-six. You have to multiply the odds for one die times the other.

Now, lets' go back to your first book of DNA information, chapter one, page one. And let's compare your page to mine in book one, chapter one, page one. What are the odds that a word in the first sentence of your page is going to look like a word the first sentence of my page?

Well, if both books used the same words, but in different places on the page (to make it simple), you might estimate that the answer is one in two hundred fifty times one in two hundred fifty, or one in sixty-two thousand, five hundred. But is it more complicated than that.

Anyway, it seems pretty remote that a word on my page one is going to be in the same place as a word on your page one.

What about a sentence on my page one? Will it look like a sentence on your page one? The odds are really climbing that it will not. What about a paragraph? What about an entire page? The odds are astronomical. Don't even think about a chapter being the same.

So, we can use probability to show that there is no one like you. Probably never was, or will be.

How can I say that there never was someone like you? Well, people are constantly changing. For instance, I went to Plymouth, Massachusetts, a few years ago. They had in their bay an exact replica of the Mayflower, the ship pilgrims sailed in as they left Plymouth, England, about the year 1620.

A lot of my folks came from England, so I felt a kinship to the people who spent so much time on that ship, even though my folks were definitely not on board. The first thing I noticed was that the decks of the ship were low. I could not fit under them for very long. Those people, both men and women, were small.

Try it yourselves. Go to a museum and look at the armor men wore in the middle ages. Most of it is too small for today's adult males. We change over time. There was most likely no one like me or you in the past.

Now, think about how our environment changes us. Our ancestors weren't raised around freeways in Southern California, with a great deal of noise and pollution. They didn't have our medicines and television and portable telephones and radios and watches and computers and on and on and on. These things change the way we react and think.

That also means that in the future, people will not be like we are. They will have all sorts of new devices and problems.

Finally, there are subtle mutations that occur in our cells. We are always subject to radiation or chemicals that will not harm us but which will cause small changes in our cells.

So you can see that each of us is truly unique. No one has ever been like us and most likely no one will be like us in the future. We are the best (and worst) version of ourselves ever in history.

Yes, I know there is one exception to all my calculations. It is identical twins. The have the same DNA because they came from one cell that split. But even *they* don't have identical fingerprints.

The next time someone tells you in a patronizing way that you are unique, get out your calculator and pencil and paper and show them how right they really are. They will never tell anyone about uniqueness again.

Relaxed Soldier guards the gold vault at Fort Knox

What Makes People Poor?

Have you ever wondered why so many people are poor? I have given the problem a great deal of thought and have read a bit and have found a partial answer. But first, let's discuss wealth.

What is wealth? Is it gold? There is a lot of gold in Fort Knox. People dug up the gold in Alaska or California and reburied it in a building in Kentucky. Did all that effort make us rich? Actually, it may have made us poorer, because all the labor that went into digging ores and processing rocks and digging holes could have been spent building houses or cars or something really useful.

Is wealth money? At any moment, our government can print all the money it wants and can give it to whomever it wants. Will that make us wealthy? No, that will only make prices rise. We know this because in Germany in 1925, the government printed lots and lots of money. There is an often-told story that a German man would fill his wheelbarrow with paper money and take it to the bakery just to buy one loaf of bread! Money lost its value quickly as the printing presses produced more of it. People had to be paid their wages every day so they could buy what they needed for that day, because money would lose some of its value by the next day.

So wealth is not gold and it is not money.

What is wealth, then? Wealth is sometimes thought of as *the means of producing something.* When a communist or socialist takes over a country, what is the very first thing it grabs for the government? That's right, the new ruler grabs all the factories. Factories produce things that people need or want. Once a man or group of men control the means of production, they are fully in control of much of the wealth of the country. Of course, they always say they are doing it for "The People," but they really own these factories for themselves.

Bill Gates and Andrew Carnegie obtained great, almost unimaginable wealth by producing things people want. Gates used Microsoft, his company, and Carnegie used U.S. Steel, his company. Computers used Gates' software, and the newly formed railroads used lots of steel. The important word is *production.*

There was a group of four young men in Liverpool, England, that were fairly good at singing and playing in their small band. They had small audiences and everyone seemed to like them. So they earned a nice, but not large, income. Once these young men were helped to be *productive,* that is, when they were helped to make records that would reach millions (instead of a hundred) and when they were made productive by being on television so they could reach even more millions, they became famous and rich as"The Beatles." None of their fame came about until they were given the tools of productivity—TV and Recordings.

So let me ask again: why are so many people poor? It is not because they are dumb or ignorant. *People are poor because they are not productive.* They have no tools, and yes, even if they had them, they would not always have the knowledge to use them. Knowledge is also a tool.

A person in a modern factory may only sweep up the floor. His tool is the broom. He usually makes a low salary compared to others. The person who runs a machine is more productive because he has a tool (a machine) and the knowledge to run the machine. His wage is often more than the sweeper's. He produces more than the sweeper.

The person who repairs the machinery in a department often has a great deal of special knowledge. He usually owns a complete set of special tools, too. He makes more than the sweeper or the machine operator. His repairs allow many machines to operate, so he is even more productive.

The tool and die maker who makes the tools that go into the machines makes even more money that all the others I have mentioned. He often spends four years in training, so his knowledge is very great. He operates many specialized tools as well. He (or she) is in a position to do much damage to expensive machinery. He is extremely productive.

The degree of productivity of the jobs I mentioned increases greatly from the sweeper to the tool and die maker.

You might note that the tool and die maker often sends his children to college. It appears that he sees the value of knowledge.

Compare these folks with a poor man in, say, Mongolia, who needs to farm so his family can eat. His needs are simple—a hoe, a shovel, and a plow. But if he is poor and cannot buy even these simple tools, he cannot be productive enough to feed his family. He is much worse off than the sweeper in a factory in this country.

Again, why is a person poor? It is because he is not productive.

Do you see why Society and your folks want you to learn as much as you can in school? So you can be productive through knowledge. Do you see a problem with drugs and alcohol? Most people using drugs and alcohol are not productive. They are in the same position as the man in Mongolia who cannot buy a shovel.

Please take every advantage to become productive. The day is not over yet.

There was a time when the kids petted Monty Python during class

The Day The Python Pooped

One of our esteemed science teachers at the high school has a pet in his classroom. It is a huge snake. It is a python named Monty, of course. I suppose Monty must be around twelve to fifteen feet long and he is big through the middle, at least six inches wide. That means he would wear a belt about a foot and a half long.

Years ago, Monty would stay very quiet until the bell rang, and then he would look around excitedly when a new class would come in. He was younger and smaller in those days, and the boys and girls would take him out of his cage and would pet him during class. He liked that. But now, he is too big, too strong and heavy to put back into his cage, so he seldom gets out unless his teacher takes him out for a "stroll."

Nowadays, Monty just dreams away the hours, with a kind of smile on his face as though he has just eaten a third-grader.

Speaking of eating, I guess you know pythons eat about once a month. And I guess you also know what else they do? That's right. They poop once a month, too.

Well, it was my luck to have to go into Monty's classroom the day he had pooped. I was his substitute teacher. It was a cool day, and all doors and windows in the place were tightly shut. Thus, the smell from Monty's cage was rather dreadful and it occupied every corner of the large laboratory. It would bring tears to the eyes of a strong man. There were dead bugs on the floor all around the cage where Monty's aroma had slain them.

What else could I do? I opened all the doors and windows and turned on the fan to suck out as much of the perfume as possible. Of course, that made the room cold. When students came in, they were cold. They rubbed their arms to reduce the size of their goose-bumps. It didn't take long for them to figure out what was going on.

As the boys and girls filed in, they asked if they *had* to sit next to Monty. I told them to find tables in the back where they would be more comfortable, and they wasted no time doing it. When class began, I checked attendance sheets and explained that Monty needed a change of underwear. But they knew that.

Then I offered to close the doors and windows if the students were too cold. They said it would be fine to leave everything as open as possible. Some of them were snacking on food they brought into the room. From this small sample of 150 students, I scientifically concluded it was just about impossible to damage the appetites of high school students.

It was quiz day. People put their minds to their tests and forgot about the odor. After the quiz, though, the first students to finish began to chat among themselves. In response, I held up a scoop I found in the front of the room and told them the noisiest talker would have to clean out Monty's cage. It was very quiet after that.

Now, why did I mention Monty Python and his problems? It is to illustrate a point. You see, most of the science and math we deal with comes from nice, neat text books. Experiments have to be simple so that a teacher can get them cleaned up for the next class.

Therefore, we become used to the "neatness" of textbook subjects.

But that is not the way of the real world. Real science and real math consist of "Python problems." Quite often, the Python poops in the world outside of our class rooms. This is the case where math problems are impossible to solve, where nothing comes out even, where our exploratory cave into an ancient tomb collapses, and where our experimental rats die of pneumonia when they are being tested for resistance to cancer cells.

That is the way life is. If everything went well, on the other hand, we would know all the answers that were important, and there would be no jobs for us when we graduate. The only reason jobs will be waiting for us in the future is because the "Python Poops" when you least expect it. Science and Math are really quite messy, unmanageable careers. That is the awful truth but also the fun of those careers.

An error message on the computer is of no use to a writer who will not read it, but has his head somewhere else.

The Scarecrow and Me

Do you remember the movie or the book, *The Wizard of Oz*? Most of us have been exposed to that story at one time or another. Do you recall the straw man, the scarecrow?

What was it the scarecrow wanted? That's right. He wanted a brain. Did the Great Wizard give him a brain? No? Well, what did he get instead of a brain? That's right. He got a college diploma. You might think a diploma is a good substitute for a brain. It is a good thing to have, but it is no substitute for thinking. And in a strange way it can help the owner, in a way not connected with getting a job.

Let me illustrate. Years ago, as someone in school about your age, I would try to read some heavy-duty science or business book. Often I would put it down and would sigh, saying, "I sure wish I were smart enough to understand what this is all about. Someday, maybe I will be able to understand it." I blamed myself when I couldn't understand what a writer was trying to say.

Later, when I had a master's degree from a good university, I would pick up the same book and try to read it. I might still have problems, but this time I would say, "Boy, that author is a bad writer!" I no longer blamed myself for not understanding what the author was trying to say. That was one of the great benefits of my college education.

You see, I had learned that some people, experts in their fields, simply cannot write! They depend on the fact that you will blame yourself if you can't understand them. Everybody who owns a pencil and paper is not a writer. Few of us are really good writers.

One of the best writers I have ever read wrote science fiction books as well as science articles. That's right, I am talking about Isaac Asimov. He could explain anything, no matter how complicated. It is a rare gift. College professors, on the other hand, are notoriously bad writers.

Besides all that, there is a saying, and I don't know who first said it, but it applies here: "Complexity is the hallmark of the half-understood." In other words, if you can't explain something, chances are that you don't understand it, yourself.

So, should you blame yourself if you do not understand all the books you have to study? Not necessarily. Sometimes we learn *in spite* of the writers of our text books. Cut yourself some slack and realize that authors of books have just as much responsibility for clarity as you, the reader, have for understanding.